THE BILLIONAIRE ROMANCE

MOST CASES ARE NOT AS BAD AS THEY SEEM, SOME HAVE HIDDEN PLEASURE IN THEM

CHAPTER 1 THE POST

Just inside her apartment door, Dalia Lindstrom dropped her bag and coat before pausing and appearing disoriented, as if unsure if she was in the proper spot.

Most days, you would have referred to Dalia as beautiful. Her face may have been a little rounder and her nose a little shorter than what the strict definitions of beauty allow, but the care she took with herself - controlling her diet to keep her body trim, expertly shaping her brows, and maintaining her fair and unblemished skin with the best (and most expensive) makeup and skin care products - was more than enough to push her over the line between "cute" and "beautiful." Of course, there was also her fabulous outfit.

But just now, Dalia's face was swollen and dark, her eyes were red, and her hair was lifeless. She wore a stylish attire that had a loose-fitting mocha knit top over skinny blue jeans that were just the perfect amount worn, along with high leather boots. She had made the choice not to weep. She wouldn't wear black for that shithead because it wasn't her colour. However, while wearing costly attire, she appeared messy, and if you looked closely, you could see some smudges on her light top.

Once she had her bearings, she kicked off her boots, took her phone from her bag, dropped it next to the luggage, and slumped into the couch. She repeatedly tapped the screen while impatiently waiting.

A caring masculine voice called out, "Dalia." "How and where are you doing?"

"At my apartment again."

"I mistakenly believed that you would be spending Christmas with your stepmother."

"Rose and I don't get along very well."

I wish I were with you in L.A. At least it's warm there, Dalia said after an awkward silence.

Another lull followed, this time lasting just long enough for Dalia to feel a threatening weight in her gut.

When your father passed away, it was obviously not the best time to have a serious conversation with Dalia about us. However, now that the funeral has passed and you are back, it is.

Her stomach grew heavier, and she asked, "What do you want to talk about, Miller?" Butterflies flitted above her tummy.

Things aren't going all that well between us, I've been thinking, he remarked. "I suppose it's time for us to, like, go our separate ways," said the speaker.

She questioned, "How are we not working, Miller?"

He remarked, "You're lovely and delightful to be with, but I don't see us as intellectually simpatico.

This was just nonsense. What does "intellectually simpatico" mean?

You don't take things seriously, I see.

Her voice, usually sweet and soft, had gone up an octave and was beginning to take on a screechy edge.

"Yes, fashion, status, being well-liked, wealth, etc.

Well, I don't currently have any money.

There you are majoring in creative writing, and you produce competent stories, but they're shallow. You're just passing the time; you're not attempting to create anything of permanent significance. But not having money won't change who you are at your core, Dalia.

My teachers adore my stories, which are good.

Technically, they're excellent—vivid characters, strong plots—but they're all about having the nicest things and the most attractive boyfriends, so you're not making art, Dalia.

Jane Austen handled it well when she wrote about the subject.

"Show it to me when you start writing like Jane Austen, and we'll chat," she said.

"I don't think so, Miller. Because, to paraphrase J. D. Salinger, what you're really telling me is that you think I'm a brainless bimbo, and you were willing to put up with me as long as I was rich and respectable, but now that I'm poor and not a trophy anymore, you don't want anything to do with me. Fuck you," Miller replied.

I'm not about money and prestige, and you know that, so that's not it.

Fuck you, Miller. Keep fooling yourself. Maybe someday you'll meet a female who's as big a fool as you are.

He groaned. "All right, Dalia, do it your way. Fuck me. I hope it all works out for you."

"I'll be alright,"

What will you do with yourself moving forward?

"Go on with my life," I said.

How are you going to survive, I mean?

I'll find employment. "I don't know yet."

"Pick yourself up and all that. That's the spirit."

Fuck you, Miller," Dalia yelled before cutting off the phone. She removed him from her contact list with a few snarling jabs of her perfectly manicured finger.

After finishing that, she reclined on the sofa and reflected on her recent chat. She had assumed she could move in with Miller when she was kicked out of her flat, so if she felt any loss, it was the loss of a resource. But she wouldn't miss him. She once had the impression that she would fall in love with him. Acting on that intuition, she gave him her virginity, but the romance fizzled out. In all honesty, she had started to see him as a pretentious bore and had been preparing to end things with him as soon as she found someone better.

His disdain was what really stung. He reasoned that she might have been the subject of Mellisa's song "Material Girl." Certainly, Dalia enjoyed lovely things. She could afford them, at least up until a few days ago, so why shouldn't she? Why shouldn't those pleasant things have made their way into her fiction? Write what you know, her teachers had instructed her, and she had done that.

She would soon be able to write about poverty, I suppose. She had enough money to cover her rent and food expenses for one month; beyond that, she would have to scavenge for food via trash diving. She was a junior in college; how would she pay for her final year's tuition? The lengthy phone conversation last week with the financial aid officer had been demoralizing. Although Dalia's high school grades were on the lower end of what they regarded acceptable, they admitted her as a legacy admission because her father, an alumnus, had been a significant donor to the university. Reminding them of his generosity didn't matter to them now that he was dead, dishonoured, and all of his money had been spent. She had all As in English but only passing grades in the other disciplines on her college transcript. With such a track record, she might be eligible for a limited aid package.

She couldn't get by on it. Even if she used all of her federal student loan eligibility and moved into a smaller apartment with multiple roommates, which is a bad idea but not impossible, she probably wouldn't be able to make ends meet. A short while ago, the rent on this Upper West Side apartment and the cost of tuition at a prestigious university seemed unimportant. Her wealthy father had paid for both. But suddenly, the sums seemed absurdly large.

It was chilly and gloomy outside. A can of soup was heated up as her poor Christmas supper. She took it to the dining room table, opened her laptop, and as she ate she looked through the Times and Craigslist job advertisements. She began out working in editorial and writing, but everyone demanded experience and college degrees, unless they were offering unpaid internships. A work in retail or the food industry would be beneficial, but the income would not be sufficient to cover both living expenses and tuition. She was in trouble any way she looked at it.

She went to Craigslist's "personals" section, which occasionally provided amusement, to cheer herself up. She grinned at the clumsy attempts to enchant in fifty words, the penis images, and the depressing longing that was visible in almost every message. She had a long way to go before she was as starved for love as these folks, even if Miller had dumped her. However, money was another issue.

She noticed a link with the age tag of sixty-two and the simple text, "Mature gentleman seeking student." She pressed. The advertisement was brief:

A mature man is looking for a college student woman for occasional company. I can assist with living and tuition costs.

She smiled, looked through a few more ads, shut down her computer, and went to bed but couldn't fall asleep. After an hour, she stood up, went back to her computer, and once more viewed the advertisement. The concept was absurd. What kind of girl would respond to such an advertisement? What sort of a man would do that? He would likely be awful—fat, drooling, oily, and odorous. She went to the kitchen and started the chamomile tea, which was exactly what she needed to fall asleep again.

Naturally, she reasoned as she waited for the water to boil, responding to that kind of ad would be similar to purchasing a lottery ticket: it was almost certain that the man wouldn't respond, and even if he did, he would likely object to the amount of money she required.

Therefore, responding to the advertisement wasn't like taking a big risk. She wouldn't be committing herself to anything, other from the almost definite fact that nothing would result from it. She could disregard any response he typed that she didn't like. Or, if she so desired, she could communicate with him via email, phone, or even meet him in a secure location; any way, it would be amusing to discuss with friends afterwards.

What if he spoke, expressed a desire for her, offered to pay, and wasn't repulsive? Well, perhaps she would. When she was a teenager, she believed that having sex would be a hugely transcendent experience, but it turned out to be merely ambiguously enjoyable, actually no better than masturbating, and loaded with little meaning. She had been simulating orgasms and having sex with a man she didn't love or even like all that much for over a year at this point. She felt no remorse and the thought of doing it with a stranger didn't repulse her.

The advertisement was still visible on the computer screen when she returned with her tea in hand. She re-read it. She found something appealing about the way the man made no mention of himself other than to imply that he was wealthy; he was far too self-assured to feel the need to tout his purported virtues, offer an explanation, or list his ideal woman.

She might also be blunt. She prepared an email and pressed the reply button.

I'm twenty-one years old, rather beautiful, and a junior in college. In your Craigslist posting, you mention a potential that interests me to talk about.

She returned to bed and eventually fell asleep after another 30 minutes. She opened her mail when she woke up at seven. There was no name in the header of the reply that was waiting for her. It just said,

Collin will serve dinner at 7:30 tonight. Do you know where this is?

On one of his visits, her father had brought her over to see Collin. If he could afford that restaurant and reserve a table quickly, he was the real deal. It was pricey and stylish. She replied, saying:

Yes, but how am I going to find you? Will you have a copy of Pravda with you?

Five minutes later, the solution appeared:

Inquire about Mr. Sane's table.

CHAPTER 2 COLLIN'S FOR DINNER

Mr. Sane didn't engage in banter, or he had never read a spy book. The dinner would likely be difficult if he lacked charisma or humour.

Whatever. Dalia had promised to leave, and she would. She spent a significant portion of the afternoon thinking about what to dress while also recovering her face and hair. She tried to appear seductive but serious, sexy but not easy. She wouldn't make fun. She ultimately settled on a straightforward light blue dress with a low cut that wasn't too low; a thin silver chain with a triangle pendant pointing downward between her breasts; and an identical bracelet. Despite making no guarantees, the clothing conveyed something about her. She created a casual updo with her hair so that it would seem stylish but modest.

Lean and straight, Mr. Sane had a formal, dry demeanour. He was not particularly handsome and had short iron grey hair and sharp, quite stern features. He was dressed formally in a grey suit. His voice reminded her of a keen knife, and instead of smiling or getting up, he motioned for her to sit in the chair across from his and stated, "You're Dalia Benitez"

She briefly wondered, "How could he know her?" She then recalled that her name would have been in the header of her email. Call me Dalia, she added with a smile.

He didn't grin back at her. "I'll call you Dalia, and you can call me Mr. Sane," he continued.

Dalia didn't anticipate enjoying him.

He asked, "Tell me about yourself."

She was careful not to divulge too much information. Mr. Sane, there's not much to tell, she added. I'm a junior who is interested in creative writing.

He continued, "I already know that, and I know you're the daughter of Millz Lindstrom, the hedge fund manager, whose fund was exposed as a Ponzi scheme, and who killed himself to avoid capture. He had taken no measures to protect his assets, and everything was seized or frozen. The man was a fool: he left you penniless.

Dalia's mood changed. Was she really that famous? Quietly, she replied, "Yes.

You may address me as Sir or Mr. Sane. Never speak to me without showing some form of deference.

She questioned why she was feeling chastened rather than outraged and replied, "Yes, Mr. Sane."

Mr. Sane asked the waiter for a bottle of Cabernet when he arrived.

"Your mother discovered him?" he enquired. "It was in the papers, but of course everyone is talking about it, too."

Sir, it's my stepmother," she said. She continued, as if it were crucial, "He was hanging from a beam in the games room; it was the only room in the house with ceiling beams."

Do you have siblings or brothers?

"No, Sir."

Uncles or aunts?

I only ever met my mother's brother once, at her funeral a long time ago. If that's what you're getting at, Mr. Sane, I don't have a family.

Dalia struggled to read Mr. Sane's expression as he analyzed her. It was difficult to keep from wriggling under his scrutiny.

Then he continued, "I've already decided that your face and body type are pleasing to me, so I invited you to dinner. Now I need to know about your sexual history and personality. Are you a virgin?"

Dalia gave him a long look. However, she hadn't anticipated him asking so soon. According to her understanding of conversational norms, an expression of sympathy was necessary at this juncture, even if it was fake. She felt heat escalating in her cheeks. No, Mr. Sane, I've had lovers before, and I slept with the last one, she replied.

"Are you still dating anyone?"

"No, Sir."

When was that over?

Sir, yesterday.

He responded dryly, "A lot has been happening in your life. Who shut it down?

He did, Sir, and he called me shallow.

Yes, he replied. "What do you mean when you say you slept together?"

She responded, unsure of what his "yes" meant and a little irritated by his interrogation, "I mean it in the typical sense." She recalled to control her annoyance: she was far from choosing to sell this man the use of her body, but she'd chosen to come here, and the least she could do was play along. Mr. Sane cocked an eyebrow, and she added, "Sir." Then, while he was thinking about making a purchase, he was only natural in his inquiries regarding the items. Take a test drive. She hoped he wouldn't insist on a road test.

Vanilla sex? he asked further. "Is there anything but vaginal penetration?"

Some oral, Mr. Sane, she whispered as blood rushed to her face.

"When you mention oral..."

She said, "I did it for him, Mr. Sane.

He said matter-of-factly, without lowering his voice, "You sucked his cock. To see if anyone was staring at them, she cast a quick peek about. Nothing was. Was that your idea, or did you comply because he requested it, he continued?

She was unsure. She reminded herself that she had the option to leave at any time because Mr. Sane's inquiries were so embarrassing. However, weirdly, she seemed to be enjoying the chat; even her humiliation had a somewhat enjoyable quality. With the option to retreat, she made the decision to continue. She said, "He inquired, Sir.

Has he entered your mouth?

As he stared at her, she felt exposed. Yes, Sir, she replied, flushing hysterically. There was no doubt that their conversation was now impacting her physically below the breasts.

Did you consume his sperm?

The query felt as though it were caressing her privates. She said, "Yes, Sir."

And that was also his idea?

I agree, sir.

Did you enjoy it?

"No, Sir."

"What about the flavour or the consistency did you not like?"

Both of those things, as well as the scent of his penis and the squirting in my mouth, were unpleasant, Sir.

You informed him that you would no longer permit him to do it.

"I didn't," I said.

Then did you permit him to repeatedly enter your mouth?

I agree, sir.

And each time you swallowed it?

I agree, sir.

Why did you continue to do it?

Now that there was an intriguing topic, it seemed weird that Dalia had never thought to ask it herself. He wanted it, Sir, and I couldn't think of a reason to say no, she said after pausing to ponder.

"Your own dislike wasn't a good enough excuse."

She was startled by his statement because she hadn't been considering those things at all. What was she contemplating? Perhaps they put up with a lot in all kinds of relationships. When she was younger, she had to kiss her uncomfortably wrinkly grandparents. She also had a high school boyfriend for a short time who believed flossing was only for pussies, but he had been the quarterback, so it had all been worth it.

I guess that wasn't offensive enough, she remarked.

He warned, "You must not forget the proper manner of address if we are to get along.

She murmured, depressed and recognizing that the sensation was accompanied by a small degree of pleasure, "I'm sorry, Sir."

The sommelier arrived with two glasses and a bottle, opened it, and poured a sample. The sommelier poured wine for the two of them after Mr. Sane sampled it and nodded.

Try the wine, Mr. Sane said.

Dalia drank a little. It tasted bitter.

Does it suit you? he inquired.

She said, "Yes, Sir."

You have to be totally truthful with me, he said. "I could tell by the look on your face that you would have preferred something different."

"Mr. Sane, I prefer whites over reds," she said.

You will sip this pricey and excellent wine, he said.

She said, "Yes, Sir." But when it would be just as simple to ask me and order wine by the glass if our tastes differ, it's difficult to understand the value of ordering something I might not enjoy.

There is a point, I guarantee you, he said. "Can you figure it out?"

She said, "I hope it's not just to make me do something I don't like to torture me." Not that the wine is really awful, sir.

"Dalia, you're on to something," he said. "Go ahead, you're doing well; there is some value in making you do something you don't enjoy, albeit there is nothing arbitrary about it."

She remarked, "Sir, you seem quite interested in power. You're setting the way power works in our relationship, if we have one, by calling me Dalia and making me call you Mr. Sane.

We do, of course," he replied. As it happens, I prefer being the dominating partner in my relationships, especially with women. "You build a relationship with every person you meet, however briefly and carelessly, and in the first moments of acquaintance you negotiate the way power will be divided between you."

When we first met, when we decided how I would address you, I said, "I understand, Sir, but why the wine too? Didn't we settle the way power worked between us at that point?"
If I order you to do something that you were going to do anyway to please yourself — read a book or order your favourite white wine — that would be an empty gesture, not an exercise of power. Power, Dalia, is fundamentally about getting people to do what you want rather than what they'd do if left on their own.
When the waiter arrived, Mr. Sane replied, "We'll both start with the squash ravioli and have the pair of beef for the main course."
"I'll appreciate those, Sir," she replied. "I hope you won't be let down,"
Not at all, he responded. While I'm thrilled that you like my decision, I'd also be happy if you didn't.
"Sir, I suppose you'd have the joy that comes from being in tune with another person's sentiments, either way," she said.
Not precisely, he answered. Take a taste of your wine, please.
She held out her glass, watching him as she did so. Although his face stayed motionless, the vivacity in his eye made it plain that he was enjoying watching Dalia sip a wine she didn't like.
He asked as she lowered her drink, "Did you pretend to like it when you swallowed your boyfriend's semen?"
I agree, sir.

Was it because you believed our pleasure would be increased if we believed you enjoyed those things—the semen and the wine—that you initially pretended to like them?

"Sir, that's correct."

I can't say I care much if you enjoy your dinner - my pleasure comes from my satisfaction in having guessed correctly about your taste in food, but I derive even more pleasure from being obeyed, especially when obedience is at its most significant - when it is difficult for you. You needn't pretend to like things to please me, Dalia. Take another sip of your wine.

When Dalia lifted the glass, it appeared to be heavy, but the closer she brought it to her lips, the more sensual the act of drinking felt; when she took a sip, she was quite certain that she was wet on the inside.

He enquired, "How do you feel?" "Be truthful."

She said, "A little turned on, Sir."

For the first time since she had first met him, he grinned. Good, he replied. Since you don't like either of these, your arousal can't possibly arise from my comparison of this wine and semen, so where does it come from?

She replied, sounding like one of Socrates' pupils, "I don't know, Sir."

"Perhaps if I rephrase it as a multiple choice question. Choice one would be that you liked those things - but we've ruled that out. Choice two would be that you enjoyed ingesting the semen and wine because doing so gave pleasure to someone else. And Choice three would be that you found pleasure in obedience itself."

I'm not sure about three, Sir. My boyfriend didn't issue commands; instead, he asked.

Instructing you to refer to me as Sir or Mr. Sane was another command I gave to you. Have you enjoyed following that order?

Dalia halted to consider her emotions. She no longer had the want to leave the situation, and she had to acknowledge that she was enjoying herself, in large part because of the type of connection Mr. Sane had constructed with its tremendous power disparity. Even if his orders were arbitrary—or perhaps precisely because they were—she had delighted in following them. They were playing a thrilling game; she had never experienced anything like it.

She said, "I've enjoyed following orders, Sir.

He replied, "Excellent," and grinned once more. You might be a good fit for what I'm doing.

If it's okay with you, Sir, may I ask what your purpose is?

He declared, "I'm seeking for a submissive."

A submissive, Sir? With restrictions, agreements, and whippings like in Fifty Shades of Grey?

He made a hand motion. "Let's just say that I am looking for someone who will accept the submissive role in a relationship. I advertised for a college student because I value youth, beauty, and intelligence, but my most important requirement is that a woman bend to my will. We would have a contract that specified limits, but in most respects that book is a poor representation of my lifestyle."

And occasionally, she said, "it will require you ordering me to do things I don't like."

You've forgotten the proper form of address once more, he remarked. Does that imply you have concerns?

"I'm sorry, Sir, but if I agree to your terms and it turns out that what you want me to submit to is intolerable, that gives you a lot of power and I won't be in a position to refuse you anything at all," the man said. "If you're going to pay my tuition and living expenses, that gives you a lot of power."

Your complete reliance on me would give me real, as opposed to hypothetical, authority, he admitted, "but our contract will limit my power, and if I break the provisions of the contract, you will have the right to cancel our agreement."

You'll be just as strong with a contract as without one. "And what would happen to me if I did that, Sir? I'd be out of money, out of my apartment, out of school, and potentially out on the street."

His smile returned. If you feel obliged to terminate the contract for cause and that person confirms you have cause, the money will be delivered to you - in a lump sum, if you wish, or in instalments - and I will place $100,000 in escrow with a third party acceptable to both of us.

If we can find someone like that, she remarked, "That sounds reasonable, Sir."
"Perhaps one of your professors; I know a lot of people at the institution," she suggested.
"Part-time companionship," your ad stated, she remarked. "Sir, how many hours is part-time?"
You'll be on call probably one or two days and nights a week, but I won't disrupt your schedule and I'll give you plenty of time to study.
This was known, but Dalia wanted to hear him say, "We would have sex, Sir."
You would grant me permission to use your body for sexual purposes, of course, and it is only fair to point out that my sexual desires are considerably more diverse than anything you have hitherto encountered.
She made the decision that now was not the time to inquire further about his sexual interests. "Sir, I'd be a whore."
If you're in a relationship with just one man, it's considered to be a "kept woman" arrangement; if you have major moral objections to that, however, this is not the arrangement for you.
Dalia's concerns weren't moral in the traditional sense. Or, to put it another way, her fastidiousness served as a reflex rather than an internalized sense of right and wrong. If Mr. Sane had been unpleasant to the touch, she would have rejected him right away. She didn't find him appealing, but she didn't find the idea of

having sex with him disgusting either because she could do it with him about as easily as she had with Miller.

"If I agree," she said.

"We'll allow two weeks for that, till, let's see, January ninth, during which time we will both be tested for sexually transmitted diseases. I dislike condoms, and I want to be able to play without them when the term of the contract begins. Do you use birth control? I'm not keen to litter the planet with brats. The only possible agreement right now is to begin contract negotiations, which may succeed or fail.

I agree, sir.

"Good. Oh, and from the moment we agree to work on a contract, you will have sex with no one but me, except as I direct you. Your body will be for my pleasure only."

She answered, "Sir," adding, "It looks not for mine either."

I will be paying for my own pleasure; yours, if you have any, will be incidental, he continued.

The waiter delivered the appetizers, and Mr. Sane barely noticed Dalia while they dined. She didn't mind because it gave her time to consider him and his proposal. She didn't like the man because he didn't have a sense of humour and didn't care much about people, at least not for her. She assumed that was the going rate for the exclusive use of a young, attractive woman who wasn't a whore yet. He was willing to pay a lot of money for sex, much of which she was almost certain not to like. Their agreement would be business-like and formal, the very opposite of what she had been taught a partnership should be.

But she was already aware of the most of that before meeting Mr. Sane. He had made it abundantly apparent in his ad that he was not looking for his true love. She had to remind herself of why she was doing this because she was poor and in need. If there was a better way to pay for her senior year of college, it was almost guaranteed to be worse than this: either becoming a drug mule or an open prostitute.

She was forced to acknowledge that this icy man's heartless proposal and something about him excited her. His conception of the submissive roused something within her that she was unaware even existed. Who was this Mr. Sane, though? She asked, "Can I ask some questions about you, Sir?" after the waiter had cleared their plates (Mr. Sane had only consumed a small amount of his).

Of course, he responded. I work as a financial consultant for wealthy clients, but that is in the nature of a hobby, and most of my income is from inherited wealth, which amounts to one to two million per year, depending on the performance of the markets. I am, in effect, one of the idle rich. You'd probably also like to know if I've made this kind of arrangement before. I have, five times over.

Do you maintain contact with any of them, Sir?"

Two of them, the prostitute and the other, occasionally send me cards, which I read but do not respond to. I keep an unobtrusive eye on them.

"Sir, you've insisted that I not have sex with anyone else. Does that also apply to you?"

"That's not exactly what I said. You won't have sex with anybody else unless I tell you to. As for me, if I have sex with anyone else, you'll know about it; in fact, you'll probably be there."

You enjoy having group sex, Sir?

We take care to secure everyone's safety, of course, and how much of that kind of behaviour you're prepared to partake in will be limited by our contract. You will have veto authority over everything. " "Sometimes, with friends and their submissives.

Can she pull this off? Her fears were being a kept lady, having group sex, and Mr. Sane's proposal. Despite the fact that she considered herself to be a person who didn't easily get excited, she was more aroused right now than she had ever been during a sexual encounter. They had eroticized the act of drinking wine through their discourse. Even her distaste for him and her apprehension were seductive. What had once seemed like a stirring inside of her was now a constant buzz. She might have been forced to do it, but she also wanted to.

Then, all right, she said. "Let's start the contract talks."

Here's to a mutually beneficial agreement, I feel we have made a good beginning, he remarked as he grinned for the third time that evening.
Of course we have, Mr. Sane. Didn't I just swallow your semen a few minutes ago? She grinned back at him, lifted her glass, and added, "Of course we have."
She took another sip of her wine while maintaining her smile and eye contact with him.

CHAPTER 3 CONTRACT EXECUTION

Mr. Sane urged that they select their neutral third party and that Dalia speak with them before making any more commitments. He gave her the option of choosing from a number of instructors who were part of the lifestyle; after some thought, she decided on Ms. Kim, an English professor with whom she had taken a class and clicked. She invited Dalia to supper at her apartment on 71st Street. She was a sweet and pleasant woman in her forties, barely five feet tall.
Instead of Ms. Kim, an attractive, thickset woman in her thirties with braided blue hair greeted Dalia at the door. She was completely naked, save for a pair of stiletto-heeled black shoes and a dark metal neckpiece.

She smiled and said, "You must be Dalia," as Dalia tried to gather herself. Please enter. My name is Lana.

Dalia was led into a living room where Ms. Kim, who was dressed casually in grey sweater and jeans, stood up from a chair and greeted Dalia warmly.

"Steven has told me very little," Ms. Kim remarked after Lana had brought a glass of chardonnay. "He suggested that you yourself describe your situation and the arrangement you're thinking about with him."

The difficulty is determining whether you're suited to it before you commit yourself. She listened intently to Dalia's story behind steepled fingers, and after it was finished she said, "The life of a submissive is strenuous. It can be one of great joy if you are suited to it; if not, it will bring you much misery."

Are you a dominant person, Ms. Kim? Dalia questioned Lana as she laid the table in the dining room while wearing an apron.

The woman responded to Ms. Kim's call of "Lana" by entering the living room and asking, "Yes, Soyuja?"

"Show Dalia who you are."

The woman responded, "I am Mistress Jang-slave," mi's and appeared appreciative of the question.

"Her servant?"

"Yes, Dalia," Lana responded with a nod.

According to Ms. Kim, "the dominant/submissive relationship can take many forms." Lana chooses to submit to my authority at all times and in all situations because she sees herself as my property.

But, Dalia argued, "she's not truly a slave."

Lana is a consensual slave because that is how our love for one another manifests itself. Thank you, Lana. You may go back to work, said Ms. Kim with a smile. "Slavery is illegal in this nation, and as a Korean, I am, for historical reasons, particularly sensitive to the topic of sexual slavery."

She gave a bow and went back to the dining room.

Dalia said, "Mr. Sane isn't into love. What he envisions is an entirely business-related transaction with no sentimental overtones.

Do you find that upsetting?

It feels like I'm selling myself, but I'm not sure I have much of a choice, so of course it does.

The fact that you're considering Steven's proposal at all tells me that you find it more appealing than the alternatives. You could take a leave of absence and reapply for financial aid when you get back. You could transfer to a less expensive school and work your way through. You could withdraw from the university and see what success you could achieve with three years of college behind you. You might be surprised.

Her gaze caught Dalia's. She was obviously correct; if she didn't do this, she wouldn't pass away in the street. She made the decision to be honest about her thoughts and emotions. I responded to Mr. Sane's ad as a kind of joke, but by the end of the evening I'd have gone home with him if he'd asked, she said. "Mr. Sane and I talked a lot about power and sex, and as we talked, I felt like he was peeling back layers of me to reveal a truer self underneath.

He's a very careful man, though, and would never ask without a signed contract in hand.

Dalia enquired, "What else can you tell me about him?"

He is well-liked in our neighbourhood, according to Ms. Kim. He is a fair but rigorous disciplinarian who upholds the terms of his contracts and his subs' agreements.

Dalia wished to know more about rules. She had not experienced many forms of punishment as a child, so the thought of facing the possibility of punishment made her uneasy. Dinner is ready, Soyuja, remarked Lana when she turned around at that precise moment.

In the dining room, Lana had prepared a Korean feast, including bean sprout soup, fish, noodles, veggies, and of course, kimchi. Ms. Kim escorted Dalia there. Lana briefly vanished and then reappeared to sit down with the other two women, donning a purple housecoat with gold embroidery that Dalia thought complemented her hair well.

Over dinner, they discussed academic life, the New York book scene, and writers and literature. Dalia saw that Lana received warm looks from Ms. Kim frequently, and he reciprocated with bashful, submissive looks that were no less warm.

They went back to the living room after supper, where Lana was once more in her undies and sat at Ms. Kim's feet, her head resting on her mistress's knee. As they conversed, Ms. Kim absentmindedly stroked Lana's hair. They were gorgeous together, and Dalia pondered whether she would ever share such emotional moments with Mr. Sane.

Oddly, there was no pain associated with the notion. Although Miller had been kind and gentle, their romance had never been particularly passionate. Due to the revelations made during her talk with Mr. Sane, Dalia had enjoyed having oral sex with him as well as making out with him. But like something doesn't mean you have to love it, be enthusiastic about it, or depend on it to give you a fuller sense of who you are. Even though she was aware that she was meant to enjoy activities like candlelight dinners and long walks in the park, she didn't feel much better after either of these experiences. Now that she had time to reflect, she realized how boring the traditional tenderness Miller had showed her had been.

What do you think, Dalia? Ms. Kim asked somewhat angrily.

She looked up at her and murmured, "I'm sorry? I'm sorry, but I got distracted.

Lana's eyes were closed when Ms. Kim asked, "Are you moving on with this scheme of yours, or have we talked you out of it?" She was slowly stroking one of her nipples.
After inhaling deeply, Dalia declared, "I'm moving through with it."
The topic of Ms. Kim's function as an unbiased third party came up. She suggested that Lana and she should split the workload, and Dalia happily accepted this. Although she had faith in Ms. Kim, she was aware that the older woman had a dominant point of view and that it would be preferable to include that of a submissive. When we talk about your affairs, Lana and I shall be on equal footing, Ms. Kim declared. They discussed a number of specifics.
The evening was suddenly finished. Dalia was escorted to the door by Ms. Kim and Lana, who both gave her hugs (it was strange being hugged by a naked blue-haired woman).
When Dalia came home, she poured a bath and took a long soak, then she went to bed and slept peacefully. The email she sent Mr. Sane simply said, "We're still on, Sir."
The terse emails they exchanged between Dalia and Mr. Sane during their contract discussions showed that they were friendly enough, but Dalia's relative inexperience made things challenging. With so little experience, how could she establish boundaries? She was able to quickly eliminate a few activities from her list, including water sports, scat, blood play, and other

extremely horrific edge play — all of which, ironically, Mr. Sane had previously informed her he didn't enjoy either. But given that she had never engaged in anal intercourse, how could she make decisions about it? She may adore it or detest it. What about public flogging? She had never even received a spanking as a kid. As a result, the contract was full with ambiguous restrictions. These restrictions included things that Dalia was frightened of but didn't find terrifying, things she wasn't sure she liked but thought she might, and things that seemed sort of gross. This category included multiple penetration, whipping, various forms of bondage, cage confinement, sensory deprivation, candle wax, and a lot more in addition to anal intercourse.

The rest of the agreement merely reiterated what Dalia had already verbally agreed to: she must be available at the designated times to fulfil Mr. Sane's sexual desires and to carry out his orders; she must treat him with the deference that belongs to a dominant from a submissive; and she must reserve her person for his sole use. He would help her, protect her from harm, and generally take care of her. The financial details of their agreement were outlined in a codicil that included the sums for Dalia's rent, the remaining tuition for the last two semesters, as well as a stipend for clothing, food, and amusement. It came to quite a sum.

When Mr. Sane and Dalia underwent their medical exams, it was evident that they were STD-free. She asked herself what sex with a 62-year-old man would be like as she renewed her prescription for birth control pills.

By Mr. Sane's deadline on Friday, January 9, the contract was prepared. She was told by Mr. Sane to sign it at six o'clock at his home in Gramercy Park. She gasped when she saw the house's three stories of brownstone. He was undoubtedly extremely wealthy if he owned that home. She checked the address a second time because she wasn't sure she had it properly.

When she rang the doorbell, he personally answered it while looking dapper in a tux. She had only ever seen him once, while he was dining, and she hadn't really noticed how slender he was. Two minutes late. You'll have to do better than that. Come in, he murmured, glancing at his watch.

He took her through a foyer into a roomy, orderly, and bright living room that featured modest but attractive furnishings, vibrant paintings and prints, and book shelves. She enjoyed this space. Six persons, including Ms. Kim and Lana (who were both properly dressed for the occasion), three males, and one other woman, were seated on a sofa and chairs. Dalia stood in the doorway gaping in shock at the sheer number of people present. She felt heavy and numb in her arms and legs. She was a little worried that Mr. Sane would force her to have sex with each of these individuals.

The man responded, "A contract like ours is not legally binding, Dalia. It can only be enforced by a community of like-minded individuals who are here to witness and celebrate our contract; the law cannot be used to enforce a contract like ours."

She grinned confidently at the people. A third man was much younger, probably in his late twenties, and was black with a muscular build, a strong, handsome face, and dreadlocks pulled into a ponytail behind. He was about Mr. Sane's age and was rather heavy; the other man was probably in his forties and was thin and elegant with prematurely grey hair. For a brief moment, Dalia found herself yearning that this man would dominate her rather than the stolid Mr. Sane. Dalia made the assumption that the third woman was Japanese, was Asian, and was only a few years older than she was. None of them were introduced by Mr. Sane.

Everyone here is aware of my dislike for formalities, so I will sign the contract first, followed by Dalia, and then the witnesses. You understand, Dalia, that after this is done, you will be under my authority.

She responded with a more than a little fluttery internal feeling, "Yes, Mr. Sane."

He uttered the word "good" before reaching into his jacket and removing the cap from a gold fountain pen. On a table in the centre of the space was the contract, which was printed on plain paper. It was open to the final Sane, which featured areas for the witnesses' signatures as well as those of the dominant and submissive. Mr. Sane walked over to the table, knelt down, and signed the papers. Dalia signed after he turned around and gave her the pen. When everyone had signed, the five witnesses stood up, gathered around the table, and passed the pen around.

The pen was given to Mr. Sane by the final witness before being placed back in his jacket pocket. Take your clothes off, he murmured as he turned to face Dalia.

She had anticipated something similar after spending the evening with Ms. Kim and Lana, but not this quickly or in front of so many people. Her face became quite hot. "Mr. Sane, I," she said.

He advised against starting the duration of our agreement with a disobedient conduct. "Take your clothes off."

She was dressed modestly in a coral dress with sheer pantyhose, simple beige heels, a white bra, and white undergarments. The dress was unzipped from behind her, and she removed it over her head before setting it on the table on top of the contract. She bent down to take off each shoe one at a time while rolling down her pantyhose while Mr. Sane observed with a blank expression. She gave him a beseeching look while standing by the table in nothing but a bra and underwear, but he was unyielding. Continue, he commanded.

Once more reaching behind herself, she released the bra's snap and took it off. She pushed down her pants and stepped out of them while attempting to avoid looking at the people in the room, who appeared to be a sizable gathering.

Turn, Mr. Sane said. "Look up: let us see your face," I said, "for everyone wants to see what I have obtained."

She slowly turned, compelled to look at the people. She forced herself to look at them since she had to be aware of them nonetheless. The Japanese woman seemed appreciative, and Ms. Kim's smile was warm and comforting. If she hadn't already been naked, you might have claimed that the youngest of the three men undressed her with his looks. They all had a sincere desire to touch her.

What do you think, Mr. Sane asked his visitors.

The Japanese woman described her as "well-formed," "attractive shape," and "medium height," adding that her modesty is becoming because it makes her nakedness even more alluring.

The young man exclaimed, "Her hair is gorgeous."

I would get one or both nipples pierced, but in a relationship of limited duration I don't believe you can require that, or tattoos, remarked the gray-haired man. "Smooth, gorgeous skin."

That, at least, was Dalia's hope.

She remarked, "I like her pubic hair," in Japanese. It's nearly velvety,

Although I think her pubic hair is nice, I think I'll have it waxed, Mr. Sane stated.

Have you seen her cunt yet? the older man inquired.

With a mixture of rage and humiliation, she reddened at his choice of words but forced herself to remain silent.

I haven't, Mr. Sane affirmed.

The man answered, "Let's see then. Make her spread for us."

To Dalia's enormous relief, Mr. Sane said, "Perhaps another day."

Dinner is almost ready, he added. Run to the kitchen and assist Khan, I said.

CHAPTER 4 THE MEAL IS SERVED

Yes, sir, Dalia said. I haven't given you permission to dress, Mr. Sane remarked as she groped for her clothes.

She inquired, "May I dress, Sir?"

No, he answered. Now hurry over to the kitchen; a good girl is there.

Although she was unsure of its location, she could probably predict where the kitchen was. She moved in that direction and quickly located it in the back of the house. At a counter, a man was slicing lettuce. He was young, tall, pale, and completely bald; upon closer inspection, she saw that he also lacked eyebrows. He was simply sporting a black collar, sandals, and an apron.

I'm Khan, one of Mistress Ai's slaves, and you must be Dalia, he continued as he turned around and grinned.

"Mistress Ai is the Japanese woman?" she questioned.

Yes, he replied.

She's gorgeous, Dalia said.

Yes, he replied. "I'm incredibly fortunate to have the opportunity to assist her."

She said, "I'm not sure what Mr. Sane wants me to do.

Khan said, "This dinner celebration is in your honour." At events like this, the submissives are always the focus of attention, but you won't be sitting at the table; you'll be serving the food.

However, she noted, "a server at a dinner party is expected to blend in."

You're not just a server; you're a nude server, and I suspect your Mr. Sane has more in mind for you than just serving, Khan stated.

She questioned, thinking if it might have been wiser to beg on the street instead of agreeing to work as Mr. Sane's sub, "Like what?"

He responded, "Hard to say. Since Sane has guests, I would anticipate some demonstration of his authority over you, but I have no idea how he will go about it. His reputation among subs is that he is a control freak who is constantly looking for ways to remind his subs who is in charge.

She questioned, "So not all dominators are control freaks?"

He replied, "My mistress isn't. "Don't get me wrong, she orders, and I love to comply, but she commands to get things done, like getting supper prepared or having an orgasm, and not just for the joy of being obeyed. And instead of backing up her commands with threats of punishment, she depends on our desire to please her."

"And that functions?"

You've seen her; that will give you some notion of what it means to be rewarded by her. "It does for me. If she appreciates this meal I'm making, she may reward me later.

Even though she wasn't totally sure she could, Dalia responded, "I can imagine."

He groaned, "If she chooses to take me to her playroom tonight, or perhaps her bed. Dalia never imagined she'd sigh in reference to having sex with Mr. Sane.

She spent the next hour serving dinner. While Lana sat next to her mistress, who fed her from her own plate and occasionally offered her a sip from her wineglass, five of the visitors sat at a large dining table. They appeared to be engaging in steamy, private behaviour.

She felt like the centre of attention, almost as if she were dancing in the midst of the table, and Khan had been right. As she served them food and beverages, everyone turned to look at her, and some of them smiled at her. She initially feared that they would touch her as she served them, but nobody did. She picked up the names she didn't previously know from listening to their chat. Eddy, Christopher, and Jerry, a young black man, were the names of the men. She paid close attention to hear more about him and discovered that he was an architect.

In the kitchen, she and Khan sneaked bites. She questioned what he was hiding under his apron to earn a name that meant "penis," but he explained that his mistress gave all of her slaves Japanese phrases as names; his meant "penis."

They called her and Khan into the dining room after she had served coffee.

It was a great dinner, Khan, said Mistress Ai. I'll give you a good reward later for it.

Dalia could see the sun radiating inside Khan as he bowed solemnly in response.

And Dalia has performed admirably on her first night as a submissive, according to Mr. Sane. Come here, Dalia; she deserves to be rewarded for that.

She moved to stand in front of him as he got up from the table. He turned around and followed her. She heard a metallic object clink. She thought handcuffs were being fastened onto one of her wrists after he grabbed it and pulled it behind her. The procedure took little longer than a few seconds, and he then repeated it on the other wrist.

He turned back to face her and murmured, "On your knees, Dalia," watching her slowly lower herself to the ground. She was relieved that she was able to accomplish this without tripping.

Mr. Sane pulled out a number of wooden sticks from his pocket. The winner will give Dalia her reward, the dominants will draw straws, he stated.

What will the prize be? questioned Jerry.

You have to make a choice, Mr. Sane said. "As long as it's not one of her strict boundaries, I'll permit anything," he said. "Perhaps you'll let her give you a blowjob. Perhaps you'll flog her or fuck her."

As she observed him travel around the table enabling each visitor to draw, Dalia's heart was pounding wildly. They all held out their straws when they were finished; Mistress Ai's was the longest.

The gorgeous Japanese woman carefully observed Dalia. Have you ever had sex with a woman, Dalia? she asked.

She shook her head and replied, "No, ma'am."

You are free to respond "No, Mistress," answered Mistress Ai.

I apologize, Mistress," Dalia responded.

Giving a woman pleasure is a straightforward process, stated Mistress Ai as she got up from her chair. "You just follow her orders," she said.

She approached Dalia and took a position in front of her while sporting a chic wraparound blue dress and black heels that she exited with far more style than Dalia believed herself capable of.

With a black coat of nail varnish and a delicate pink cherry blossom painted on each toenail, Mistress Ai slid one foot forward. You're welcome to kiss my foot, she said.

Dalia could bend over without losing her balance if she sat back on her heels. The foot of Mistress Ai, however, was about six inches away. Before she could get there, she had to uncomfortably shuffle forward on her knees. She quickly kissed Mistress Ai's instep while being conscious of everyone's attention before sitting up.

You lacked excitement, according to Mistress Ai. "Perhaps my foot has to be cleaned; do it for me. Then we can kiss more comfortably."

Dalia gave her a perplexed look. With her hands restrained behind her, how was she supposed to wipe her foot?

Dalia, with your tongue," she commanded.

As she knelt down once more and tentatively licked her instep, Dalia was hot all over.

Mistress Ai declared, "All over." Why not start at the ankle and work your way down to the toes?

To reach her ankle, Dalia had to advance a few more inches. Switchbacks were made as she walked back and forth. The toes took a few minutes to clean, and Mistress Ai fanned them out, advising, "Don't forget to scrub in between."

Being appreciative that Mistress Ai's toes were immaculately clean, Dalia licked between them. When Dalia had completed that chore and was relieved that it was accomplished, Mistress Ai elevated her big toe and commanded Dalia to "suck my toe."

How long will this misery last? Dalia nervously regarded Mistress Ai's attractive toe.

Mistress Ai responded with a kind, "Go ahead, Dalia." I'm sure you must be an eager cocksucker, so just pretend it's a cock.

The remarks of Mistress Ai cut. In her burning face, her breasts, her tummy, and down below, where she was immediately aware of her bottom high behind her and her sex exposed to everyone's gaze, Dalia felt the shame. She worried that Mr. Sane may shove her from behind and, to her surprise, she didn't find the idea repulsive.

This toe was just as beautiful as the rest of Mistress Ai's; the nail was delicately painted, the skin was white, and there were no calluses. Its beauty shocked Dalia. She pushed forward with a piercing whine, her mouth shut over Mistress Ai's toe, and she sucked.

Dalia assessed her emotions when Mistress Ai's toe was in her mouth. Though she was unable to see them, she was aware that everyone in the space was watching her intently and taking pleasure in the sight of her crouched on the floor, wrists bound behind her, adoring an elevated being while completely naked.

Did they intend for her to be unhappy? If so, this submissive was defying them since every cell in her body appeared to be on fire with pleasure, and her heart was singing with joy. If she could, she would suck Mistress Ai's toe all night.

However, after a little interval, Mistress Ai told Dalia, "That's enough. You can kiss my foot again and see if it's more to your taste."

Now that she had grown to like Mistress Ai, Dalia kissed her foot tenderly where the toes met the instep. She stood up and awaited the subsequent humiliation.

What more would you like to do? What would make you happy? Would you like to give me cunnilingus? asked Mistress Ai.

Dalia was opposed to doing it. She had been stealing looks at Mistress Ai during dinner because she thought the woman was stunning, but the thought of kissing and licking her sex repulsed her. She understood that she would still do it joyfully and without hesitation. What caused that?

She said, "I would like to carry out your order."

Dalia said, "That's a great response, Mistress Ai. You obey your dominant by following me, so stand up.

She was able to stand up without toppling over and, in her opinion, with a fair amount of grace. Mistress Ai approached her, placed her hands on her shoulders, and then gave her a long, tender kiss that made her feel hot.

After taking a step back, Mistress Ai knelt down, picked up her shoes, and then she sat back down.

Eddy said incredulously, "Is that all?" Look at these three fine subs, Arty. My cock is throbbing; let's take 'em downstairs and play for a while. I thought we were going to be treated to some cunt-licking.

Mr. Sane said, moving behind Dalia to release her handcuffs, "Another day." "I'm afraid I'll have to call it a night early."

All right, Eddy said with a knowing grin. I understand. Thanks for the food, and have a great night.

They all wished Mr. Sane good night. While Ms. Kim and Lana hugged her, Khan shook her hand, Eddy, Christopher, and Jerry gave Dalia a quick glance without saying good night. Mistress Ai also smiled warmly at her.

She then had her new dominant to herself. Pick up your clothes and follow me, he murmured, leading her upstairs.

He pointed to a door and said, "You may sleep in that room. He gestured to a door on the opposite side of the hall, "You'll find everything you need in there, and it has an adjoining bathroom.

She had spent the evening naked, being stared at by strangers and near strangers, and finally sucking a beautiful woman's toe, so she was keyed up. She hadn't exactly been looking forward to sex with Mr. Sane, but she was reconciled to the necessity of doing it, and she was resolved to do it well and with conviction, giving him a good experience.

However, after responding "Yes, Mr. Sane," she walked towards the door.

Dalia," he said.

She turned to face him once more.

Don't schedule anything for the morning or the evening of tomorrow, he advised.

She hesitated for a moment and then said, "Yes, Mr. Sane. May I ask you a question, Sir?

You are always welcome to ask me questions, and I will choose whether or not to respond, he said.

His face was pallid and twisted, with skin that was tightly stretched over the bone. "The game you had them play tonight, about rewarding me," she replied. I was curious how far you would have permitted them to stray.

"Mistress Ai and I determined in advance it would be ideal tonight," he said. "It was head play, Dalia. There will be body play afterwards.

So they fixed the straw draw so Mistress Ai would win, Sir?

She grinned, for some reason finding the concept appealing.

The exhaustion in his eyes was almost startling. "Every game you play with me will be rigged, Dalia," he finally concluded. "Now get some sleep." He was motionless for a few seconds, as if gathering his courage to speak.

Five. In Dalia's bedroom

A simple white cotton nightgown was in the closet, and the bathroom was well stocked with new toothbrushes and a few common brands of toothpaste, soap, and shampoo: not the brands she used, but good enough. The room Mr. Sane had directed Dalia to sort of a guest room, furnished with plain but good quality furniture, with few signs of personality anywhere, and inoffensive artwork on the walls.

She took a shower, put on her nightgown and panties, and tried to fall asleep, but she couldn't help picturing Mr. Sane naked and wondering what he would want from her: would he lie back and demand that she serve him, or would he be more active? Would he be as reserved in bed as he was at other times? She tried to push the images and questions out of her mind, but she couldn't.

Her father, tanned and fit, was stretching by the edge of the pool while Rose read on a chaise nearby. In her dream, she was lying out in the sun behind the family home, asking her father, "Am I doing the right thing, Dad?

"Microsoft 27.97, up $37 cents, GM 38.02, down $6 cents, Bank of America 978.00, down $8 dollars, and DuPont 21.78," he responded. . Angry, she exclaimed, "Motherfucker! He flailed in the water as she lunged at him and pushed him into the pool, but he kept eluding her. "Here, try this," Rose said as she handed her a leaf skimmer with a long handle, which she used to jab him under.

Her wrist was tightly grasped. "No!

He fucking deserves it, she sobbed.

She attempted to shake the hand away, but it was somehow tying something to her wrist with a clasp.

She opened her eyes and saw Mr. Sane, dressed in a white shirt and dark slacks, fastening a soft leather cuff to her left wrist after tying one to a bedpost on her right.

"Mr. Sane? She responded, "Sir? "

He shackled her left wrist to the other bedpost and instructed her to only speak when spoken to.

"I'm not going to injure you, Dalia," he murmured as he grabbed her left ankle, dragged it wide, cuffed it, and placed it somewhere beneath the bed-frame. He then circled the bed and did the same with her right ankle.

He lifted the hem of her nightie and peered below. Now her legs were spread wide, like a ballerina's split.

You will no longer wear underwear in this house, he added, pointing to the panties you were wearing. To acknowledge what I say, you may speak.

I get it, Sir," she replied.

He took a folding knife from his pocket, opened it, sliced her panties on each side, and pulled them off, dropping the remains on the floor and standing thinking about his work. He did all this with quick, dexterous movements - there was no hesitation or shyness in him, but rather the sureness that comes from the conviction that you have an absolute right to do what you want with what is yours.

She tightened her eyelids while he worked because she felt a rush of terror.

His eyes met hers briefly and then strayed over her body, not with a hungry look, but with appreciation and satisfaction, as if she were a painting he'd just won at auction, Dalia lifted her head to see him sitting beneath her left foot, relaxed, legs crossed, with a mug of coffee on a small table beside him.

"Sir?

", said her.

Dalia, be quiet, he said.

She wanted to use the restroom to relieve herself and to brush her morning breath away because what if he wanted to kiss her? But she would have to wait until later.

Minutes passed. She occasionally heard the sound of his mug being set down on the wooden tables and pondered what more he may be planning to do with her body since there was a big list of things he was allowed to do, some of which would be painful. She questioned whether he preferred to focus on one aspect of her body over others, such as her breasts, face, hair, or sex, and felt warm down below as a result of his gaze, which wasn't weird, sly, or shameful.

He stood up from his chair, moved two steps to the side of the bed, held her eyes, placed his palm on her sex, and used his middle finger to probe into her cleft as if it were a cue.

He said, "You're soaked, Dalia."

She acknowledged that she was wet and muttered, "Mmm," thinking that she could get away with it.

She moaned as he put another finger into her and pushed harder and faster until the stimulation was almost too much, turning pleasure into pain - and it was painful, the way his fingers were pounding her full bladder. He slipped his finger inside and gently stimulated her, gradually increasing tempo and force until she could hear the liquid slopping of his finger.

She whimpered, "Oh, please," and tried to wriggle free of his grip, but she was unable to do so and he was relentless; her whole body trembled under the weight of him. She could hardly think for the overwhelming sensation; her pleas turned into a shrill keening; and she thrashed on the bed with the hope that if she pulled against her cuffs hard enough, she might be able to escape.

When she finally recalled the safe word, she was about to yell, "Red!

When he came to a stop, he leaned over her, released her right wrist and ankle, grabbed her arm, and rolled her toward him while still holding onto the bed frame with one hand and one foot. She was lying on her side at the edge of the mattress when he did this.

Before she could react, his hand caught her attention and unhurriedly moved towards his zipper, grasping the tab with two fingers, and slowly pulling it down. He reached into his pants and pulled out his penis, which he stroked languidly just a foot from her eyes, making himself hard. She was shocked; she'd never been handled so roughly before.

She had known from the beginning, below the level of conscious thought, that this would be the opening act, the first thing he'd want, and he'd want it often because he knew she didn't like it; and she'd love it and need it because... because.

She opened her mouth to receive him and let him push into her - deep, too deep! She coughed and spluttered, and when he drew back, she spat out a mouthful of drool. He held himself with his right hand, put his left hand behind her head, fingers sunk deep in her luxuriant hair, and pulled her towards him.

She spit out more thick saliva and opened up again for the next onslaught as he pulled back just before she would have lost her breakfast, if she had any. He was now grasping the back of her neck and he plunged in again, and she gagged and her stomach gave a lurch.

She put her free hand on his belt buckle to push him away because this wasn't the oral sex she'd discussed having with Mr. Sane for Miller, the slightly unpleasant cock sucking followed by a little spurt; this was an assault where he was using her head as a sex-toy and caring less about how she felt about it than if she were made of plastic.

However, she realized that she had been craving this all along, even at Collin's house where she had wet her underwear while drinking wine: not the sensation, stimulation of a mouthful of warm flesh and the churning stomach, but being used in this manner: without sweet words, a kiss on the neck or a tender caress - without acknowledgment of her human dignity even - but with a primal sexuality that knows what it wants, is certain of what is due to it, and

She twisted a nipple hard as he attacked again, deeper this time, pulling her roughly into him, forcing her wide open - and somehow she was adjusting to this treatment, not gagging as much or as afraid of throwing up, but focused on her raw emotions, her impossible arousal, her hand sliding down her belly to her sex, where she found her climax. She was made to be ravished like this: why had she never known it before?

Until he took two handfuls of her hair, held her motionless while he backed away by a single inch, and pumped his warm, sticky semen into her mouth.

She swallowed hard, forcing it down, rolled onto her back, and looked at him, waiting for what would happen next. He withdrew from her and pulled her head back by the hair so he could watch with flat eyes what he knew she would do without his commanding her - what she dreaded doing and needed to do.

What's in your head, Dalia? ", Mr. Sane finally asked after putting himself away, zipping up his pants, and retiring to his chair. He had been silently observing her for some time.

She paused, astonished by the inquiry, and added, "I'm thinking it's strange, Sir, that a man who doesn't care whether or not I enjoy my dinner wants to know what's on my mind right now."

"Careful, Dalia," he urged. "Insolence will not be rewarded."

"I'm not being insolent, Mr. Sane," she responded, voice loud and quavery. "I'm being honest, the way you taught me to. I'm genuinely curious about this. Do you care what's going on inside my head? "

I'm curious, Dalia, he said. Now respond to my query.

"How are you interested, Sir?" she asked. Are you hoping that I'll say it was awful so you can enjoy my suffering? Unfamiliar, unexplainable feelings were seething inside her; she was crying.

She noticed him tense a little, looking irritated, and said, "This is what's in my thoughts, Sir."

I don't want you to be miserable, Dalia, he added.

I appreciate it, Mr. Sane.

"I need to find out. . . what you're thinking," he said.

She sniffled and added, "Sir, I need to urinate.

He stood up and released her handcuffs while appearing exhausted. Come back immediately after, he instructed.

She hurried to the restroom, thanked everyone, and sat down to relieve herself. As she relieved herself, she took a big breath. After she had finished, she went back to the bedroom and stood beside the bed after rinsing her mouth with water.
Do you intend to tie me up once more, Sir?
"Not at this time."
She faced him while sitting on the edge of the bed. She waited for him to speak while her breasts and sex were heated and her entire body glowing.
He demanded, "Well."
I haven't had an orgasm, Mr. Sane, but I'm incredibly turned on.
Masturbate, he instructed.
She fixed her gaze on him. He sat in his chair motionless.
Are you staying here, Sir?" she inquired.
"Yes. You must be aware that when within this residence, you have no right to privacy."
She replied, "Maybe I'll simply wait till later, Sir."
It was an order, he claimed. "Masturbate."
She paused, then stroked herself while still seated by dividing her legs. She softly stimulated the somewhat covered clitoris by massaging her labia with her flat, joined fingers.
It felt extremely good, but was it her hand or his fixated gaze on her hand and genitalia that was arousing her? Together, hands and eyes undoubtedly, and her left hand as well because it had

somehow made its way to her right nipple and was squeezing and twisting it.

She worked while gazing at Mr. Sane, her mouth slightly open and gasping for air. His features (a powerful face, only beginning to show signs of ageing) were fixed, but his eyes were alive, his erection already roaring back. He was like a coiled spring when he sat up straight.

He abruptly stood up from his chair. He gave her a hard push in the back, bouncing her head off the mattress. His lips closed over her, his tongue, rigid as a penis, probed into her wet slit, slid upward, and slammed into her clitoris. He batted her hand away, fell to his knees as he elevated her legs, and did all of this in one continuous motion.

She wanted to writhe away because there was too much stimulation, but she was restrained by his hands on her thighs, which held her just as tightly as her binds had before. As if what he was doing to her wasn't enough, she bit her knuckle and rough-kneed it.

When her orgasm finally occurred, it was a tremendous, crashing sensation unlike anything else she had ever experienced. She continued to scream for an unknown amount of time until it was over, at which point she collapsed tired with her bare feet hanging down, unsure of when she would have the strength to stand up.

Mr. Sane got up and silently walked out of the room. In less than a minute, he was back with a big plaid bathrobe, which he set on the bed next to her.

"Put this on, and come to the kitchen, he instructed. You can find something to eat for breakfast while I make some fresh coffee."

Yes, she agreed. She wants to eat breakfast.

CHAPTER 6 THE MAXIMUM PENALTY

At the kitchen table, they dined in silence. He had a lot of questions Dalia wanted to ask, but his demeanour made communication difficult.

Dalia was wondering what would happen next as they were wrapping up when Mr. Sane added, "You and I have a scheduled appointment at J. Sisters for 11:00. You have the afternoon to do as you choose."

She said, "Yes, Sir."

Now, take some Advil, he advised. "This will lessen the discomfort of waxing. It is located in the cabinet next to the stove on the right."

She replied, "Thank you, Sir," and walked over to the cabinet he had indicated. She took a moment to realize the Advil was hidden inside a "Gleevec 400 mg" pill bottle. She took two Advil tablets from the container and shook them out before returning to the table and taking some coffee to go with them.

About ten was the time. He said, "You'd better get ready and depart." "Being early won't do any harm. Dinner will be served here at six."

She inquired, "Am I going to serve?"

For the fourth time throughout their interaction, he grinned and stated, "Dalia, no. You will be the main course this time."

She had never had a Hollywood wax before, so the staff at J. Sisters weren't exactly on board with it, but she insisted they do it anyway because that's what she'd been taught to do. Her skin would be sensitive for a few days after the treatment, which nearly caused her to pass out from the discomfort.

She walked to Rockefeller Plaza after her appointment and ate lunch at Just Salad. The apparel and accessories, which she typically found so fascinating, received little of her attention as she spent the afternoon wandering through the Midtown shops. She was engrossed with thoughts of her odd dominance and the last twenty-four hours' worth of events. She was captivated by the paradox that despite not liking them and having to do them, she adored the things that had been done to her. She was lost in thought during her meditations and had to sprint to the Lexington Avenue train. A scowling Mr. Sane opened the door to the Gramercy Park residence at around six fifteen.

He stated: "Both times you've visited this residence, you've been late. Follow me here."

Following him to the back of the home, Dalia felt more than a little uneasy as he unlocked a door that led to a finished basement room that contained various tools that she had read about and seen online, including a St. Andrew's cross, a cage, a bondage table, and more. Looking at those items in images is one thing; being in a room full of them is quite another. It spooked me.

She said, "I'm sorry, Mr. Sane. "I won't allow that to occur again."

He said, without glancing at her, "Strip."

She took off her clothes fast.

He pointed to the cross and said, "Over here." He then chained her hands and feet so they were facing the wall and tightened her cuffs so she was hung and unable to touch the ground with her toes.

She watched as he entered a closet and reached inside to get a black whip with several tails, each measuring about two feet in length and ending in a knot. He turned to face her with his expressionless gaze.

The cosmos appeared to reconfigure itself as he got closer, with the whip at its centre. She was instantly reminded of the horrible welts that slaves' backs had in old photographs. She would die if that were done to her since she couldn't stand it! Her breath became quick and shallow as her heart pounded within her. Her body erupted with energy, and she desperately strained at her handcuffs in an attempt to escape.

She said in between wheezing, "No. "No!"

As Dalia writhed on the cross, looking wildly, trying to flee from him like a fox in a trap, Mr. Sane paused and peered at her. She shouted as he took one more step.

She had the sensation that her chest might break. She yelled, "No! No! No!" before adding, "Please, No!" and "No!" She made a terrible raspy sound as she tried to breathe as her body twisted on the cross and she was unable to continue speaking because she ran out of oxygen.

After a brief period of standing motionless, Mr. Sane dropped the whip, dashed to the cross, and freed her feet and hands. She collapsed to the ground, gasping for air in loud gulps; she buried her face in her shaking hands; and as soon as she could breathe again, she began sobbing hysterically, her shoulders heaving and her body trembling as if she were crouched naked in a snowdrift rather than on the warm basement floor.

She made an attempt to say "No," but the word eluded her.

A gentle, hesitant hand was placed in the middle of her back, and she overheard a voice resembling Mr. Sane's but lacking his steely edge.

The voice yelled, "Dalia!" "Dalia! This is done."

Where had the blanket that was covering her come from? - and the voice began to speak while the hand stroked her back "Dalia, it's done. That's it."

Slowly, she regained control of her body and consciousness. She finally whispered the safe word, "Red," as her panic gave way to basic dread.

"Yes, Dalia, I do. I know, "Mr. Sane remarked.

I'm sorry, she sobbed. I'll stop being late, I promise.

I am aware of it, Dalia," he said.

He allowed her to dress when she was able. When she was seated at the kitchen table, he went and retrieved the contract after bringing her up to the kitchen and making her tea. She watched as he pulled out his gold fountain pen, crossed out "flogging," added it to the list of "strict boundaries," and then crossed it out again.

She received the contract and the pen after he initialled both locations in the margin. She signed with a hand that was now only slightly trembling.

Did you anticipate acting in such a manner at the sight of a whip, Mr. Sane asked?

No, Sir, she answered. "However, I suppose I don't deal with pain well. When they were waxing me today, I almost passed out."

Would you rather skip the waxing this time?

I'm not sure, she said. I'll consider it, Sir.

This is why I occasionally need to ask you how you feel, he continued. "I don't intend to torture you. In fact, if you'd prefer, we don't even have to continue with our agreement. Do you wish to continue, please?"

Dalia fixed her gaze on the boiling tea in her mug. She paused for a moment to collect her thoughts as Mr. Sane patiently waited. Finally, she exclaimed, "Was I supposed to resent the things you did to me last night and this morning, Sir?"

He stated: "You should have felt a certain degree of dislike, but a great deal more pleasure, if I judged you correctly, and you're actually a submissive, not simply a girl in need of money," the man said.

Do you believe that you can be content without... without beating me, Sir?

"For me, this is all about control," he declared. The actions themselves don't matter all that much because it's a mental game. Some dominants have different feelings. However, I would be content if we closed the door to my dungeon and never went inside."

"Sir, I liked the cuffs. If the crucifix and the other items can be used for something other than whipping, I could appreciate them."

She shivered, but this time it was delightfully. "They have various purposes," he added with a frigid smile.

Dalia smiled and inquired, "What's for supper, Sir?"

He just so happened to have several containers of warm Chinese cuisine sitting in the kitchen from his refrigerator.

Mr. Sane demanded, "Tell me about your writing."

She remarked, "Sir, most of my writing is like these high school romances. "They were considered unimportant by my ex-boyfriend, and perhaps he was correct. I was heeding the suggestion to write about what you are familiar with."

Mr. Sane questioned, "Do you think that's good advice?" "After all, very few science fiction writers have visited Tau Ceti, and the majority of authors of detective novels have never worked as detectives. Even though Chaucer claimed he was incapable of love, some of the best love stories ever written are some of his."

Sir, maybe you're right, Dalia said. "Even though my professors enjoy my stories, I've been growing tired with them. It could be time to move on. Though I'm not sure where I'll get my ideas from."

"There is inspiration all around you, Mr. Sane continued, in books, newspapers, and daily life. What books do you enjoy?"

They discussed novels well into the night. Mr. Sane was a voracious reader but had never attempted to write anything. Even though he had a stern demeanour, she found that conversing with him was fascinating and motivating since he gave her the impression that she could actually write a novel. She agreed to send him some of her work via email.

It's time for bed, Dalia, Mr. Sane said somewhere after midnight. She wished he'd bring her to his room and let her stay there. She wanted him to bind her and give her a fuck. But he repeatedly sent Dalia to the room across the hall from his, and each time she was let down because he appeared to have forgotten his promise to make her the dinner's main entrée.

If you're not up now, I'll wake you up at eight, he said.

Looking at him, she wondered whether there was anything she could do to make him want her. She noticed the same tiredness in his face as the previous evening, as well as the illusion that he had aged ten years in only one hour.

She inquired, "Are you all right, Sir?"

Get some rest, he advised.

She got up at seven in the morning, got ready, had a shower, and went downstairs to the kitchen. There, she looked around until she found everything she needed for coffee and a straightforward breakfast of toast and scrambled eggs. When he showed up around eight, she was prepared. He ate some of the meal she had prepared, though it was hard to tell if he appreciated her initiative.

He said, "When they're done, "Now you can return home. Bring extra clothing for the weekend and return on Friday at six o'clock."

She said, "Yes, Sir."

To the foyer, he noticed her. He picked up and gave her a tote bag that was at the door.

He said, "There are instructions inside. Before you come back, "Follow them precisely."

She said, "Yes, Sir."

He inquired, "Do you have cab fare?"

She hesitated, comparing the amount of money she had left in her bank account to the amount she required for supper. She replied, "I'll take the subway, Sir."

He answered, "Here," pulling out several folded and clipped bills from his pocket. She received two twenty-dollar bills from him. She took the money from him even though it felt odd and wrong in some sense.

She would have felt better with an embrace or a kiss, at the at least on the cheek, but he didn't make that move, and she didn't believe it was her place to make that type of contact. She gave him one last look before leaving the house and heading to Park Avenue to call a cab.

She took the tote bag into her flat and opened it. A leather pouch with three silicone butt plugs of various sizes and a blue silicone dildo in the form of a penis were both inside. She discovered a lubricant bottle and an envelope with a note inside, which she presumed was written using Mr. Sane's gold fountain pen. The note said, in part:

Until you can fully insert the dildo, practice oral sex. Online resources for guidance are available. Start with the tiniest plug to train your anus (you must use lubrication), and when you feel comfortable there, advance to the next size. The largest one should be comfortable to wear for an hour at a time.

She took her laptop and all of stuff to her bedroom out of curiosity. She disrobed, lubricated the tiniest butt plug, and gently inserted it. She was happy that it felt good rather than painful.

She opened her laptop while wearing the plug and searched for "practice deep throat." After viewing a few films and reading numerous web page with enthusiasm, she got to work. She slipped the dildo (water-based, unflavored, non-toxic) in until she felt her gag reflex start to activate. She then tipped her head back and pushed out her tongue. She took a breath, waited, collected herself, then made another attempt. She quickly came to the conclusion that Mr. Sane hadn't really penetrated her all that far in the morning and that she still had a lot to learn before she could deep throat like the women on the videos.

Her mouth and throat were in line as she lay on her back with her head hanging over the edge of the mattress. She immediately became highly aroused because she thought Mr. Sane was leaning over her and pushing into her. She took a moment to place the next size butt plug. Though not nearly as much as the waxing had hurt that morning, it still ached.

Once more lying down, she inserted the dildo and revelled in its twin sensations with the plug. If Mr. Sane's cock was in her throat, then perhaps Jerry, the charming young architect, was in her ass, and the two of them were utilizing her body in concert.

After a few minutes of massaging with an open hand, she inserted two fingers.

Mistress Ai was now utilizing her body, with a strap-on dildo in her pussy, Mr. Sane in her ass, and Jerry's cock in her throat. None of them cared about her humiliation or dignity; they were only interested in having fun in her open holes.

She had an intense orgasm that left her shaky and exhausted.

CHAPTER 7 THE NIGHT

Dalia read, wrote, and practiced with her butt plugs and dildo every Friday night the next week. After sending a small sample of her works to Mr. Sane, she had an idea for a story unlike any other; it was about a young couple who survive by begging in the subways. The girl must decide how to survive once the man left her. Although Dalia was unsure of the plot's direction, she enjoyed the idea and put a lot of effort into writing a compelling opening scene.

By Friday, January 16, she had mastered wearing the largest butt plug for an hour and was able to easily raise the dildo to the flared base. She gave herself plenty of time to get to Gramercy Park, where she strolled through the neighbourhood carrying her overnight bag until just before six o'clock, when she rang Mr. Sane's doorbell.

A attractive woman in her forties who was wearing black boots, a black leather jacket with steel studs, black slacks, a black top, and black boots opened the door. She had several piercings in her ears and an eyebrow piercing with a stainless steel ring. She smiled and continued, "Mr. Sane has excelled himself this time," giving Dalia a grateful nod.

Since Dalia was accustomed to praise, she grinned and replied, "Thank you."

"The woman answered, "Well, you'd best come in," and when Dalia was safely within the foyer and the door was shut, she introduced herself as Molly Carter. You can call me Molly, even though Mr. Sane calls me Mrs. Carter. I work as his cleaner, and no, I've never had sex with him. At home, I have a fuck toy of my own."

Dalia, who had grown fond of Molly right away, requested to be called Dalia.

Molly added, "Mr. Sane wants you to undress here in the entryway. "I'll take your suitcase and clothing for you," she said.

Dalia removed her frock (she had worn no underwear as per Mr. Sane's orders) and her shoes, wondering if she would ever get past her self-consciousness about being naked.

He wants you to wear this, Molly added, pointing to a little table that held a hand towel, a tiny bottle of lubricant, and a metal butt plug with a jewelled end, which Dalia could see. The plug matched the largest one Mr. Sane had ever given her in terms of size.

"Okay," responded Dalia, knowing well that she was about to suffer some major humiliation.

Molly responded, "You don't want me to watch you put it in." I'll wait on the opposite side of that door, she said. Beyond the foyer, she vanished into the corridor.

After lubricating the plug and her anus, Dalia knelt down and entered it, groaning at the brief coolness of the metal. After washing her hands, she crossed the doorway to stand next to Molly.

She muttered, "Do you know what he's going to do with me?

She responded, "Sorry, no," and then ushered her into the living room, where Mr. Sane was seated alongside Mistress Ai and Jerry. Both of the men were dressed in suits, Mr. Sane's a charcoal colour and Jerry's a light grey that complemented his delicious deep brown skin tone. Mistress Ai was dressed in a stunning pink and white silk kimono.

Although she was giddy with anticipation, Dalia stood in the centre of the room not knowing what was expected of her.

Jerry remained silent while gazing. No hello kiss for me, Mistress Ai grinned and cocked her head.

Mr. Sane, who was watching with curiosity, caught Dalia's eye.

If Mr. Sane authorizes it, she said.

He said, "You may kiss Mistress Ai."

Still hesitant, Dalia regarded the attractive Japanese woman.

Then what?" asked Mistress Ai.

How would Mistress Ai feel about being kissed, Dalia enquired?

Mistress Ai enquired, "What type of kiss do you prefer the best, Dalia?"

Dalia gave it some thinking. When Mistress kissed her on the lips, it was incredibly enjoyable. When Mistress kissed her feet, it was exciting in a different manner, and Mistress had hinted at another kind of kiss—one that was sexier and more intimate. However, the type of kiss wasn't really important.

Dalia remarked, "I enjoy the kisses that Mistress reserves for herself.

With a loving smile, Mistress Ai got up from her chair and said, "Dalia, that is a really good response. You are a lucky substitute for Steven."

The wide sash was undone by her as she reached behind her, pulled it off, and set it down on the chair. She unzipped her kimono, took it off her shoulders, and let it float behind her into a glistening pool.

She was now completely naked, graceful and slim with perfect, little breasts and tiny nipples. Above her right breast, a vivid dragon tattoo stretched its mouth widely and curled sensually across her shoulder. Dalia gaped in amazement.

Mistress Ai moved closer to Dalia and used a thin finger to trace the contour of her mouth. "Such lovely lips, pink and shaped, she exclaimed. They are designed to be kissed."

She grabbed Dalia's hand and drew her to the chair she was occupying. She placed her delicate hands on her shoulders and forced her to her knees with absolutely no force. She stood up and put one foot on the arm of the chair, allowing Dalia to see the smooth pink labia and the soft, straight, and short black pubic hair of the Mistress directly in front of her between her parted legs.

Dalia had always been particular about her own sex up until about a week ago, when Mistress Ai brought up cunnilingus. Although she occasionally masturbated, she didn't appreciate the taste or fragrance of her own body. When she touched herself, she never licked or sucked her fingers, and she always carefully cleansed them afterward. However, she has been masturbating every day since last week and licking the moisture off her fingers in an effort to grow accustomed to it.

"Kiss me, Dalia," said Mistress Ai as she placed a hand on her head and her fingers in her hair while pulling her forward.

Dalia tilted her head back and tentatively kissed Mistress Ai's sex. When she was close to it, the taste and smell were much more potent than they were on her fingers. She yearned to stand up and leave. Use your tongue, Dalia, or I may believe you're not happy to see me, warned Mistress Ai as she firmly held her in place.

As Dalia's tongue glided into Mistress Ai's warm, wet crack, her stomach lurched uncomfortably. However, Mistress let out a lovely, breathy "Oh," and with that, Dalia's entire body began to sing with joy and pleasure. She took a deep breath and noticed that Mistress had a musky, clean scent that wasn't foul or slimy, and that she was moist with active passion. Dalia devoured it with eagerness.

Too quickly, Mistress Ai reached into Dalia's thick hair, yanked her head aside, and peered into her eyes. She told her, "You kiss beautifully," and pushed her to the ground on her back. Dalia felt her sexual warmth surge as she dipped down over her head, crushed her exposed pussy on her mouth, and humped her.

Dalia was ready to reach for her own pussy while completely engrossed in her feelings and sensations when strong, sure hands—which Dalia knew to be Mr. Sane's since they exuded a confidence that could only be his—grabbed her ankles and lifted her legs. A cock slid into her wet vagina as she felt a man's warm thighs against her lower half.

The dreams she had been experiencing all week about having the dildo in her throat and her fingers inside her were a thousand times worse than this. Dalia's cheeks were saturated with Mistress Ai's juices as she rode her face faster and harder. The butt plug inside of her was already moving as a result of Mr. Sane's forceful thrusts, which also stimulated her anus.

Mistress' fingers were still in Dalia's hair, and she was screaming—first, a soft scream as she ground herself repeatedly into Dalia's lips and tongue for what felt like a full minute—in a high-pitched, rhythmic cry of approaching orgasm. Eventually, her body relaxed.

Dalia was kissed and had her hair petted by Mistress Ai after she climbed off her face. Now that Dalia could make out who was between her legs, Jerry watched with interest while remaining seated. The elder man fucked her while inattentive to her and preoccupied with his own sensations. The thought that he was paying so little attention to her and caring so little about her pleasure thrilled Dalia and somehow made the sensation of him inside her even more intense. Dalia adored watching him, still in his grey suit (did he never get naked?).

When Mr. Sane arched his back and walked over while panting, she could feel her own orgasm starting to develop and was almost there. This, in Dalia's opinion, was the drawback of having a boyfriend who was not sensitive to her feelings: she wouldn't always be able to go.

Mr. Sane emerged from Dalia shortly after Jerry handed her a towel to mop up the drips.

Standing up, Mr. Sane tucked himself away. He muttered as he zipped up his pants, "What a waste of the appetizer. Dalia, head to the kitchen and inquire as to when supper will be served from Mrs. Carter."

Mistress Ai was donning her kimono, but Dalia refrained from asking to get dressed. After returning to the kitchen, she uttered, "Hello Molly! Mr. Sane is curious about the status of supper."

Molly said, "I don't understand why he cares. "He only takes one bite at a time. Tell him to wait for fifteen minutes."

They were all seated at a little, square supper table after fifteen minutes. Even though Dalia was still naked, sitting on her butt plug was painful. Jerry was to her left and Mistress Ai was on her right.

Tonight, Jerry hadn't said much; perhaps he was shy. He appeared to be unable to respond to Dalia's attempts to converse with him. Instead, Dalia was restless and bored as Mistress Ai took control of the conversation by presenting news and guiding debate about people who were familiar to everyone present but her.

The moment Mr. Sane finally moved his chair back and said, "Come back to the living room with me. For our post-dinner entertainment, Mrs. Carter is welcome to bring us coffee or other beverages."

A futon had been set in the centre of the living room floor by someone, most likely Molly. Dalia, please stand on the futon, urged Mr. Sane. Then he spoke to the crowd. "Last week, I handed Dalia two homework tasks. One was to get her anus used to taking a big butt plug for an entire hour. I can tell she finished that one since she inserted a plug of that size when she walked in tonight and has been wearing it ever since. Dalia, squat down so everyone can see your butt plug."

She stooped to reveal her plug to Mr. Sane. She then made a gradual spin so that everyone could see. She enjoyed the little surge of shame she had after flashing her ass with the pornographic diamond in it.

Mr. Sane declared, "The second task she was given was to learn how to deep throat a dildo. Dalia, did you carry it out?"

Yes, she said, "Mr. Sane."

"Unfortunately, I neglected to request that you bring the dildo back so that you could show off your new ability. You didn't bring it by chance, did you?"

"No, Sir," Dalia said. "I apologize."

"We'll just have to get by. "No issue, Steven," responded Jerry when asked if he would mind allowing Dalia to suck his cock "Jerry uttered this and got to his feet.

Jerry was more like Mistress Ai, who had undressed to play with Dalia before dinner, if Mr. Sane preferred to have sex while still wearing his clothes. He leisurely removed his jacket, tie, shoes, pants, and other accessories until all that was left was a gold wristwatch. He had a slim waist and a fine, well-muscled body. His skin was dark with copper highlights. As he made his way near Dalia, he gripped his penis in his palm and rubbed it. Now that he was nude and in his element with a thickening cock, all of his dinnertime shyness had vanished. Dalia believed she had never seen a body so exquisite and thought he was an Adonis.

At the futon's edge, he came to a stop. She knelt down in front of him and gazed at his cock, which had a shaft that matched his body's rich brown colour and a circumcised head that was lighter in colour with a hint of pink. She took him in her hand, lifted him, and licked the length of his shaft from his balls to the very tip. She teased his slit there before taking him in her mouth very slowly as the dark head, then the corona, and finally the darker shaft all vanished between her pale pink lips.

She took him slowly in order to prolong their enjoyment for each other as well as Mr. Sane and Mistress Ai, who were keeping careful tabs on them. Before she extended her tongue to kiss his balls, she waited for her lips to make contact with his shaved base.

Clapping his hands, Mr. Sane exclaimed, "very good However, deep throating a dildo or Jerry when he is still is one thing. When something is moving, it becomes entirely different. You know what to do, Jerry."

After pulling away from Dalia, Jerry knelt down and gave her a quick kiss. "Lie down, babe," he whispered, guiding her to a face-up position with her head pushed back and off the end of the futon.

Jerry crouched over her and carefully lowered himself into her mouth, doing so until he was well within and her nose was mashed against his balls. Then he pulled out a few inches and pushed in again, this time more quickly after a few repetitions. He used longer, harder strokes until her mouth was overflowing with drool, which then went into her eyes, across her forehead, and into her hair. She couldn't help producing an odd quacking noise that astonished and worried her as he was fucking her faster and deeper, the slick sound of cock resounding in her ears. But what a sensation, to be treated this way! His hands were on her breasts, massaging her nipples, and as he strained into her, his brown asshole flexed an inch from her eyes while his hard balls bounced. Her hand landed on her pussy below, and she vigorously stroked it.

Someone was pushing and dragging the butt plug in her ass, fucking her with it, and then finally yanking it out of her. Her ankles were lifted by hands as a warm cock pushed into her ass. What else could it be but Mr. Sane's cock? She could feel the man's assurance and his mastery in the way he held her and thrust. She was stretched by the butt plug, but that didn't stop the discomfort. She hummed around Jerry's large cock because she was unable to speak up in opposition.

Stretching painfully, she finally felt pleasure from Mr. Sane's smooth skin rubbing against her anus. Now that his rhythm and Jerry's were in sync, Dalia felt Mr. Sane's hard thrust into her from below jolt her entire body; similarly, when Jerry shoved into her throat, it pushed Mr. Sane deeper into her ass, amplifying the sensations there.

Though Dalia could only see Jerry's supple and muscular ass, it had to have been Mistress Ai's fingers that had pushed her hand away from her pussy and pushed into her there. As she rubbed and squeezed her nipples, all of her erogenous zones were stimulated, causing waves of sensation to crash throughout her body.

She had no idea how long it would be before Jerry arrived, filling her mouth to the brim with thick spurts before a drip escaped and ran over her cheek. She saw Mistress Ai with her fingers in her pussy and Mr. Sane fucking her ass when he got off her. She ingested Jerry's sperm, which combined with the pleasure of seeing Mr. Sane and Mistress Ai as well as the stimulation of her pussy and ass, caused her to experience an even greater orgasm than the one she'd had the week prior when masturbating for Mr. Sane.

Dalia fixed her gaze on Mr. Sane, whose hooded eyes swept over her face admiringly but failing to see past the expertly applied makeup. At this moment, she had no interiority for him; she was nowhere to be found. Good, she said. She wanted to be his plaything at the time, but later they could converse about life and literature.

With a few quick strokes, his semen arced over her belly and splashed on her breasts, chest, and neck after he pulled out of her ass, giving her sphincter a jolt of pleasure. He gave her a quick look before getting to his feet. He answered, "I'm going to put myself away and zip up." "How are things doing with that new office building, Jerry? Again, where was it? Saint Louis?"

CHAPTER 8 THE SHORT BREAK

After midnight, Mistress Ai and Jerry departed. He collapsed into a chair in the living room when Dalia and Mr. Sane returned from taking them out. Dalia realized at that moment that he had been struggling to maintain his composure for hours and was now exhausted.

Sir, can I assist you?" she asked.

He said in a voice barely above a whisper, "Go to bed, Dalia."

"Sir, I could bring you a snack or a beverage. I could assist you with the stairs."

"Go to bed."

"Sir . . ."

"Don't try my patience, Dalia," he snapped.

She said, "Yes, Sir." "Good night, Sir."

He didn't answer.

In her room she found her overnight bag beside the door. She hung some things in the closet and took out some toiletries, which she carried to the bathroom. She drew a bath and had a long soak: the warm water soothed her sore anus.

She went to bed, but sleep wouldn't come. The evening had been too exciting. She'd been there and not there, the centre of attention and a mere thing for them to use. Everyone had fucked her; they had used her and abused her, perforated and slimed her, and it had been gross, but its grossness had turned her on. And, strangely, they had loved and respected her even as she'd been a thing for them. They'd understood her needs and cared enough to meet them along with their own.

But Mr. Sane worried her. When had she ever seen anyone so tired as he had been the two evenings she'd spent with him?

It came back to her in a flash - a memory from when she was just nine. Her mother, dying of breast cancer, had been that tired, and she'd become thin and pale. It was as if a huge hand were closing around Dalia's heart.

What was the name of that medicine she'd seen in Mr. Sane's kitchen cabinet? She took her phone from her bag and Googled "Gleevec."

She stayed up till three in the morning, reading and rereading web pages.

Mr. Sane woke her at eight, not by tying her up but with an invitation to breakfast, which he was making himself.

"I'm not a bad cook, when the mood strikes," he said. Was it just her imagination, or was there a glimmer of cordiality in his manner this morning?

She sipped coffee and watched him fry sausage and bacon and make toast and home fries. He brought her a plate heaped with food.

"This looks delicious, Mr. Sane, but it's about four times as much as I usually eat," she said. "Will you be insulted if I take like one bite of each thing?"

"If I were Christian Grey, I'd take you to the red room of pain and cane you," he said.
"Thank God you're not Christian Grey, Sir," exclaimed Dalia. "After two weeks with him, I'd be a sow."
I'm not a food addict, he declared. "I doubt that I could eat more than you do."
After one minute of quiet, Mr. Sane said: "You had good stories. They have genuine talent, and their sense is something to get to know. They brought back sad recollections of embarrassing moments and the awkwardness of adolescence from my own school days. Tell me what you're currently writing."
She gave him her opinion on the panhandlers on the subway.
He said, "I like it. "Do you believe a wealthy man who supports the girl in exchange for sex will save her?"
Dalia uttered, "The idea is overly idealistic. Nobody would think that."
Mr. Sane laughed, and it was clear what he was laughing at despite its peculiar, cutting cough. Both surprised and delighted, Dalia.
She stated: "Although I'd like to save her, I believe she needs to continue to descend before she can escape by climbing out. Prostitution. possibly drug abuse possibly more Homeless people on the streets experience horrible things."
He sadly responded, "I suppose so. Funny how fiction frequently makes people feel worse off than in real life.

If it weren't for you, Sir, my life would be very difficult.

"You'd be fine. It might be a little harder."

Dalia asked, "May I ask more about you, Sir?" When you're not reading, gambling with other people's money, or abusing women's bodies, what do you do?

He remarked, "There's not much to say. "I'm a really boring guy. I watch TV, read, and have meals with friends."

Do you have children?

He questioned, "Why do you want to know?"

I'm intrigued, Dalia remarked. "We are in a connection. It makes sense that others would want to know more about you."

Ask another question, he advised.

Do you have siblings or brothers?

"Dalia!"

"You asked if I was the only person in the world, Sir. I need to know right now if you are."

"I enjoy my alone time. In any case, I have you."

But, Sir, you don't treat me like a member of your family, a lover, or even a friend.

"We've discussed writing..."

You won't even say, "Sir, do you have a family?"

"Our contract doesn't say I have to be open with you," she said.

"Maybe you need more right now, Sir, than what the contract says. I've only been your sexual object for a few days, and while I've been really happy, I'm worried about you."

You express concern.

"concerning your health, Sir. your persistent leukaemia."

"How did you learn that?"

"Sir, I haven't been nosy. However, I couldn't ignore how exhausted you are, and when you asked me to get some Advil last week, I noticed that you were also taking Gleevec."

"You'll be taken care of if I pass away, Mr. Sane stated icily. You need not be concerned."

She became enraged. Do you really believe that all I care about is money, sir?" she questioned.

If I weren't paying, "you wouldn't be here," he said.

"You're sure I see you as just a James, and I'm just a whore to you, she continued. You've never kissed me because of this. A whore isn't given a kiss. You only touch her as much as is necessary."

"Dalia, I don't think of you as a whore."

"So, Mr. Sane, stop treating me like one. Even though our relationship is only business-related, treat me like I can care about your wellbeing."

Mr. Sane dipped his head and tightened his nose bridge, appearing to be gathering his patience.

He commanded Dalia, "Go home." "Be unconcerned about me. I'll be alright."

He wasn't going to be alright, in Dalia's opinion. His leukaemia was growing, if she understood what she had read; she was worried. 'Your symptoms, Sir,'

Dalia, you're not a doctor, he said. 'Go home.'

Shall I return on Friday?" she enquired.

Yes, he replied. "Next Friday. Details will be sent later."

Mr. Sane wrote Dalia on January 21 to let her know she wouldn't be needed that weekend. She was dissatisfied because she had been anticipating serving as Mr. Sane's and perhaps more of his friends' new favourite sex toy once more, but she could wait another week. She toyed with the dildo and butt-plugs he had given her before purchasing a vibrator from a sex shop in the city centre, oblivious to the salesperson's ravenous expression.

The following week, Mr. Sane once more had to cancel, and Dalia began to worry. She alternated between being convinced that he was abandoning her and being confident that his health was deteriorating. The following week, she received her rent payment and a check for living costs as normal, but he omitted to extend an invitation to his home. I hope you're doing well, Sir, and that I haven't upset you, she wrote in a letter to him. I long for our meetings.

He didn't reply via email. However, the thought of calling him terrified her.

The next week, she wrote Mr. Sane once more, asking if they could talk about it if he was upset with her. That is the proper course of action in both professional and interpersonal relationships.

On February 6, he replied, saying, "I'm not mad with you." You'll be informed when you're needed. Your help will keep coming.

CHAPTER 9 MR STONE

The instructor of Dalia's advanced fiction writing class, Mr. Stone, declared, "This narrative is a major departure for you." He was a tough novelist in his fifties with chiselled features, and Dalia had felt honoured to be accepted into his class. It had been more than three weeks since she had last seen Mr. Sane; it was Tuesday, February 11.

Dalia said, "I hope it's okay, Mr. Stone." She was concerned that he would tell her that her narrative about the subway panhandler was unacceptable when he called her into his office following class. She had eloquently described how her James, a lean sixty-two-year-old man, had taken her orally and anally at the scene where Stella pulled her first trick.

Naturally, it's acceptable, Mr. Stone said. "It's fantastic, in fact. Though they are more about you than the plot, I do have some worries. Of course, we are all aware of your father and your predicament. I'm very sorry about everything. Such a great loss, and it's not even your fault. After reading your narrative, it occurred to me that it could be a result of your own sense of abandonment or the loss of your family and/or support system."

She snorted and said, "I have to urinate, sir.

He seemed fatigued as he rose up and unfastened her restraints.

He told me to come back right away.

She quickly went to the bathroom, thanked everyone, and then sat down to use the restroom. She exhaled deeply after using the restroom. She rinsed her mouth with water and then went back to the bedroom where she stood next to the bed.

Do you plan to bind me again, Sir?

"Not right now,"

She sat on the side of the bed and looked at him. She heated her sex and her breasts as she waited for him to speak, her whole body glowing.

Well, he demanded.

Mr. Sane, although I haven't experienced an orgasm, I feel tremendously hot.

He told me to masturbate.

She kept looking at him. He didn't move while he sat in his chair.

Do you intend to stay here, Sir? "She questioned.

"Yes. You must understand that you have no right to privacy inside this house."

"Maybe I'll just wait till later, Sir," she retorted.

He said it was a directive. "Masturbate."

After pausing, she divided her legs and continued to sit while petting herself. She gently massaged her labia with her flat, joined fingers, stimulating the slightly covered clitoris.

It felt great, but was she being aroused by his fixation on her hand and genitalia or by her own hand? Together, hands and eyes obviously, but also her left hand because it was gripping and twisting her right breast and had found its way there for some reason.

Her lips was slightly open and she was gasping for oxygen as she worked and looked at Mr. Sane. His features, a strong face that was only starting to age, were fixed, but his eyes were animated, and his erection was already roaring back. When he sat up straight, he resembled a coil of spring.

He suddenly got out of his chair. He pushed her firmly in the back, which caused her head to jump off the bed. His tongue, which was as stiff as a penis and closed around her, slid up into her moist slit before slamming into her clitoris. He swatted her hand away, dropped to his knees, raised her legs, and did it all in one fluid motion.

Too much sensation made her want to writhe away, but she was held back by his hands on her thighs, which held her just as securely as her bonds had. She bit her knuckle and gave it a rough-kneed bite as if what he was doing to her wasn't enough.

When she eventually had her orgasm, it was a powerful, jarring sensation unlike anything else she had ever felt. When it was ended, she screamed for an undetermined length of time before collapsing exhausted with her bare feet hanging down and wondering when she would have the strength to rise up.

Mr. Sane stood up and quietly left the space. He returned in just a minute carrying a large plaid bathrobe, which he placed on the bed next to her.

"He said, "Put this on, and come to the kitchen." While I brew some hot coffee, you can find something to eat for breakfast."

She said, "I agree," She desires breakfast.

They ate quietly at the kitchen table. He had many questions, but his demeanour made it difficult for Dalia to communicate.

As they were closing up, Dalia was wondering what would come next when Mr. Sane said, "J. Sisters has set an appointment for us for 11:00. The day is yours to spend however you like."

Yes, Sir, she said.

He said, "Now, take some Advil." "This will make waxing less painful. It can be found in the cabinet to the right of the stove."

She gave him a "Thank you, Sir" response and went to the cabinet he had pointed out. It took her a while to realise the Advil was concealed within a bottle of "Gleevec 400 mg" pills. Before returning to the table and getting some coffee to go with them, she took two Advil tablets from the jar and shook them out.

The hour was around ten. You'd better get ready and leave, he remarked. "It won't hurt to arrive early. At six, dinner will be served here."

Am I going to serve? she asked.

He smiled, and for the fourth time in their conversation, he said, "No Dalia. This time, you will be the main dish."

The staff at J. Sisters weren't exactly on board with her getting a Hollywood wax because she had never had one before, but she insisted on it nonetheless because that's what she'd been taught to do. After the therapy, her skin would remain sensitive for a few days, which nearly made her faint from the pain.

After her visit, she strolled to Rockefeller Plaza and had lunch at Just Salad. She spent the afternoon perusing the shops in Midtown, paying little attention to the clothing and accessories, which she usually found so fascinating. She was preoccupied with her peculiar dominance and the happenings of the previous twenty-four hours. She was fascinated by the paradox that she loved the things that had been done to her despite not wanting to do them and having to do them. She had to run to the Lexington Avenue train since she became disoriented during her meditations. Around six fifteen, a scowling Mr. Sane flung open the door to the Gramercy Park home.

He declared: "You were late both times you came to my house. Observe me here."

Following him to the back of the house, Dalia felt more than a little uneasy as he unlocked a door that led to a finished basement room that had different items, including a St. Andrew's cross, a cage, a bondage table, and more, that she had read about and seen online. Being surrounded by those objects in person is very different from seeing them in pictures. It frightened me.

I'm sorry, Mr. Sane, she said.

That won't happen again, I promise."

"Strip," he ordered without giving her a second glance.

She quickly removed her clothing.

"Over here," he said, indicating the cross. She was then hanged and unable to touch the ground with her toes because he tightened her cuffs and chained her hands and feet so they were facing the wall.

She observed as he went into a closet and pulled out a black whip with multiple tails, each of which was about two feet long and knotted. He turned to look at her with a blank stare.

As he neared, the universe seemed to rearrange itself, the whip at its centre. She was immediately brought back to mind the hideous welts that slaves' backs had in old pictures. If that were done to her, she would die because she couldn't take it! As her heart raced through her body, her breathing became rapid and shallow. Her body erupted with energy, and she struggled mightily to get free of her restraints.

She spoke while gasping, "No. "No!"

Mr. Sane halted and glanced at Dalia as she writhed on the cross, gazing madly and attempting to escape from him like a fox in a trap. As he took a further step, she yelled.

She felt as though her chest may rupture. "No! No! No!" she screamed, followed by "Please, No!" and "No!" She struggled to breathe as her body twisted on the cross and she was unable to speak further due to oxygen deprivation. She made a dreadful raspy sound.

After briefly remaining still, Mr. Sane threw down the whip, sprinted to the cross, and set her feet and wrists free. As soon as she was able to breathe again, she collapsed to the ground, gasping for air in loud gulps while hiding her face in her trembling hands. She then started sobbing hysterically, her shoulders heaving and her body trembling as if she were naked and crouching in a snowdrift rather than on the warm basement floor.

She tried to say "No," but she couldn't get the word out.

In the middle of her back, she felt a soft, tentative hand and heard a voice that sounded like Mr. Sane's but lacked his steely edge.

"Dalia!" shouted the voice. "Dalia! It's finished."

What was the origin of the blanket she was wrapped in? - and while the hand stroked her back, a voice began to speak. "Dalia, it's completed. I'm done now."

She gradually regained awareness and control over her body. Finally, as her fear gave way to simple dread, she muttered the safe word, "Red."

"Dalia, I do, I do. I know, "Sane made a comment.

She wailed, "I'm sorry. I swear I'll stop being late.

Dalia, I am aware of that "said he.

When she was able to, he let her get dressed. He brought her up to the kitchen and made her tea, then went and got the contract when she was seated at the kitchen table. She saw him take out his gold fountain pen, cross out "flogging," put it on the list of "tight restrictions," and then cross it out once more.

He initialled both places in the margin and handed her the pen and the contract. Her hand was now only barely trembling as she signed.

Mr. Sane questioned, "Did you foresee doing such a thing at the sight of a whip?"

She said, "No, Sir." "I guess I don't handle pain well, though. I nearly fainted today while they were waxing me."

This time, would you rather forego the waxing?

She replied, "I'm not sure. Sir, I'll think about it.

This is why I need to ask you how you feel now and then," he said. "I have no desire to torture you. In fact, we don't even have to keep with our arrangement if you don't want to. Would you like to proceed, if possible?"

Dalia's eyes were glued to her mug of steaming tea. Mr. Sane kindly waited while she took a time to gather her thoughts.

Was I expected to be angry at you, Sir, after what you did to me last night and this morning? she exclaimed.

He said: "You're genuinely a submissive, not just a girl in need of money, and you should have felt a small degree of aversion, but a great deal more pleasure, if I judged you correctly."

Do you think you might be satisfied without... without punishing me, Sir?

This is all about control for me, he said. Since it's a mental game, the actions themselves don't really count all that much. Different dominants experience various emotions. However, I would be happy if we left my dungeon's door closed and never entered."

"I liked the cuffs, sir. I could respect the crucifix and the other objects if they may be utilized for something other than lashing."

This time, she shuddered in a lovely way. With a cold smile, he said, "They serve a variety of purposes.

What's for supper, Sir? Dalia asked with a smile.

Unexpectedly, he had many warm containers of Chinese food in his refrigerator that were currently being served in the kitchen.

Please tell me about your writing, Mr. Sane commanded.

"Sir, most of my work is like these high school romances," she commented.

My ex-boyfriend thought they were unimportant, and maybe he was right. I was following the advice to write on subjects you are knowledgeable about."

"Do you think that's good advice?" Mr. Sane inquired. "After all, very few authors of science fiction have actually been to Tau Ceti, and most writers of detective fiction have never been detectives.

Even though Chaucer insisted he was incapable of love, some of his works have some of the greatest love stories ever recorded." Dalia answered, "Maybe you're right, sir." "My teachers seem to appreciate my stories, but I'm becoming bored of them. Perhaps it's time to move on. Although I'm not sure where my inspiration will come from."

"Mr. Sane went on to say that you can find inspiration in books, newspapers, and everyday life. What are your favourite books?"

They talked about books long into the night. Although Mr. Sane read a lot, he had never tried to write anything. Despite his severe demeanour, she found talking to him to be interesting and inspiring since he made her feel like she was genuinely capable of writing a novel. She consented to emailing him some of her work.

After midnight, Mr. Sane said, "It's time for bed, Dalia."

She wished he'd take her to his room so she could spend the night there. She wanted him to tie her up and screw her. But despite promising to make her the dinner's main course, he kept sending Dalia to the room down the hall from his, leaving her disappointed each time.

He said, "I'll wake you up at eight if you're not up already."

She questioned whether there was anything she could do while she studied him to make him want her. She saw that he still looked exhausted from the previous evening, and that he appeared to have aged ten years in just one hour.

Are you okay, Sir? she enquired.

He suggested that you rest.

She rose at seven, dressed, had a shower, and then made her way downstairs to the kitchen. She searched the area until she discovered everything she required for coffee and a simple breakfast of toast and scrambled eggs. Around eight, he arrived, and she was ready. It was difficult to tell if he appreciated her initiative, but he did consume part of the food she had made.

When they were finished, he stated, "Now you can go home. Bring extra clothing for the weekend, and come back at 6:00 on Friday."

Yes, Sir, she said.

He saw her walk into the foyer. A tote bag was by the door, so he picked it up and presented it to her.

He stated: "The interior has instructions. "Follow them exactly" before you return.

Yes, Sir, she said.

Do you have cab fare, he asked?

She paused, weighing how much cash she had in her bank account against how much she needed for supper. I'll take the metro, Sir, she retorted.

He said, "Here," and reached into his pocket to reveal numerous folded and clipped notes. He handed her two twenty dollar dollars. Even though it seemed strange and inappropriate in several ways, she took the money from him.

He didn't make that move, and she didn't think it was her place to initiate that kind of contact, so she would have felt better with an embrace or a kiss, at the very least on the cheek. Before leaving the house and going to Park Avenue to summon a cab, she gave him one more glance.

When she got inside her apartment, she opened the tote bag. Inside was a blue silicone dildo in the shape of a penis and a leather pouch containing three silicone butt plugs of varied sizes. A lubrication bottle and an envelope with what appeared to be a letter written with Mr. Sane's gold fountain pen were also found by her. Part of the note said, "Practice oral sex until you can fully insert the dildo." There are resources for guidance available online. To train your anus, start with the smallest plug possible (you must use lubricant), and when you are comfortable there, move on to the next size. The biggest one ought to be bearable for an hour at a time.

Out of curiosity, she brought her laptop and everything else to her bedroom. She took off her clothes, oiled the smallest butt plug, and then carefully inserted it. She was relieved that it didn't hurt, but rather felt fantastic.

While still using the plug, she opened her laptop and performed a search for "practice deep throat." After seeing a few movies and enthusiastically reading a lot of online Sanes, she started working. She injected the water-based, unflavored, non-toxic dildo until her gag reflex began to work. She cocked her head back and stuck out her tongue after that. She exhaled, waited, composed herself, and then tried again. She quickly realized she hadn't actually been penetrated by Mr. Sane all that deeply in the morning and that she still had a lot to learn before she could deep throat like the women in the movies.

She was lying on her back, her head hanging over the edge of the mattress, her mouth and throat lined up. She was instantly very excited since she believed Mr. Sane was putting pressure on her and looming over her. The following size butt plug was inserted after a little pause. It still hurt, though not quite as much as the waxing had stung that morning.

She inserted the dildo while still lying down and savoured its complementary pleasures with the plug. Perhaps Jerry, the charming young architect, was in her ass and the two of them were using her body in concert if Mr. Sane's cock was in her throat. She massaged with an open palm for a few minutes before inserting two fingers.

With Mr. Sane in her ass, Jerry's cock in her throat, and a strap-on dildo in her pussy, Mistress Ai was now making use of her body. Each of them merely cared about having fun in her open holes; they didn't care about her shame or dignity.

She experienced a powerful orgasm that left her fatigued and unsteady.

The following Friday nights, Dalia read, wrote, and practiced with her butt plugs and dildo. She had an idea for a narrative unlike any other after emailing Mr. Sane a short sample of her writings. It was about a young couple who make their living by begging in the subways. After the man went, the girl must decide how to survive. Despite being unclear of the plot's course, Dalia liked the concept and worked hard to write a gripping first scene.

By Friday, January 16, she was able to lift the dildo to the flared base with ease and had perfected wearing the biggest butt plug for an hour. She arrived at Gramercy Park with plenty of time to spare, carried her overnight bag through the neighbourhood, and waited until just before six o'clock to knock on Mr. Sane's door.

The door was opened by a striking woman in her forties who was dressed in black boots, black pants, a black shirt, a black leather jacket with steel studs, and black boots. She had many piercings in her ears and a stainless steel ring pierced her eyebrow. Dalia received an appreciative nod as she grinned and continued, "Mr. Sane has exceeded himself this time."

Dalia smiled and responded, "Thank you," as she was used to receiving compliments."

When Dalia was safely inside the foyer and the door was closed, the woman said, "Well, you'd better come in," and then identified herself as Molly Carter. Although Mr. Sane refers to me as Mrs. Carter, you are welcome to call me Molly. I work as his housekeeper, and no, we have never had sexual relations. I have a fuck toy of mine own at home."

Immediately falling in love with Molly, Dalia asked to be called Dalia.

"Mr. Sane wants you to strip here in the foyer," Molly continued. I'll transport your clothing and suitcase for you "She spoke.

In compliance with Mr. Sane's orders, Dalia took off her dress and her shoes. She wondered if she would ever get over her embarrassment over being naked.

Molly continued, pointing to a little table that contained a hand towel, a tiny bottle of lubricant, and a metal butt plug with a jewelled end that Dalia could see. She said, "He wants you to wear this. The plug was identical in size as the biggest one Mr. Sane had ever given her.

Dalia said, "Okay," knowing full well that she was going to experience some serious humiliation.

You don't want me to watch you put it in, Molly retorted. She said, "I'll wait on the other side of that door." She disappeared into the hallway beyond the entryway.

Dalia lubricated both the plug and her anus before entering it, grunting at the momentary coolness of the metal. She wiped her hands before stepping through the threshold to stand next to Molly.

She grumbled, "What is he going to do with me, do you know?

Sorry, no, she said and led her into the living room where Mistress Ai, Jerry, and Mr. Sane were seated. Mr. Sane's suit was charcoal, whereas Jerry's was a light grey that suited his lovely deep brown skin tone. Both of the guys were dressed in suits. Gorgeous pink and white silk kimonos were Mistress Ai's choice of clothing.

Dalia stood in the middle of the room, thrilled with anticipation but unsure of what was required of her.

Jerry stared without saying anything. Mistress Ai cocked her head and smiled, "No greeting kiss for me."

Dalia noticed Mr. Sane, who was observing with interest.

If Mr. Sane gives his approval, she said.

You may kiss Mistress Ai, he said.

Dalia looked at the gorgeous Japanese woman, still unsure.

Next, what? "questioned Mistress Ai

Dalia asked, "How would Mistress Ai feel about being kissed?"

What kind of kiss do you like the best, Dalia? asked Mistress Ai.

Dalia thought about it. It was so much fun when Mistress kissed her on the lips. Mistress had hinted at another kind of kiss—one that was sexier and more intimate—when she kissed her feet, and it was exciting in a different way. The nature of the kiss, however, wasn't particularly significant.

In Dalia's words: "I like the kisses Mistress saves just for her.

Mistress Ai stood up from her chair and grinned warmly "That is a really excellent response, Dalia. You are a fortunate stand-in for Steven."

She reached behind herself, pulled the wide sash off, and laid it down on the chair. She removed her kimono off her shoulders, unzipped it, and let it float into a sparkling lake behind her.

She was suddenly graceful, thin, and entirely naked, with exquisite, little breasts and tiny nipples. A bright dragon tattoo that coiled sensually across her shoulder and spread its mouth widely was inked above her right breast. Dalia gaped in shock.

Mistress Ai approached Dalia and traced the outline of Dalia's mouth with a slender finger. "She remarked, "What exquisite lips, pink and formed. They are intended for kissing."

She took Dalia by the hand and drew her over to the chair she was sitting in. With no force at all, she pushed her to her knees by placing her delicate hands on her shoulders. The Mistress was immediately in front of Dalia between her opened legs as she got up and placed one foot on the chair's arm, allowing Dalia to see her silky pink labia and her soft, straight, short black pubic hair.

Prior to Mistress Ai bringing up cunnilingus approximately a week ago, Dalia had never been picky about her own sex. She performed some masturbating, but she didn't like the taste or smell of her own body. She never licked or sucked her fingers when she touched herself, and she always washed them gently afterwards. She has been trying to get used to it, though, by masturbating every day since last week and licking the moisture off her fingers.

Mistress Ai pulled Dalia forward and said, "Kiss me, Dalia." She put a hand on her head and her fingers in her hair.

Dalia leaned back and cautiously kissed Mistress Ai's genitalia. The taste and fragrance were much stronger when she was near to it than they were on her fingers. She wanted to get up and go.

Mistress Ai cautioned Dalia as she was tightly held in place, "Use your mouth, or I may feel you're not happy to see me."

Dalia's gut lurched uncomfortably as her tongue slipped into Mistress Ai's warm, moist crevice. Nevertheless, Mistress uttered a sweet, breathy "Oh," and at that moment Dalia's whole body started to sing with delight. She inhaled deeply and discovered that Mistress was moist with intense excitement and had a musky, clean aroma that wasn't unpleasant or slimy. Dalia eagerly gobbled it up.

Mistress Ai jerked Dalia's head back too soon, looked into her eyes, and reached into her thick hair. "You kiss beautifully," she said before pushing her to the ground on her back. As Dalia dropped over her head, pressed her exposed pussy on her mouth, and humped her, she felt a burst of sex.

Completely lost in her sentiments and sensations, Dalia was about to reach for her own pussy when strong, sure hands—hands that Dalia knew were Mr. Sane's because they projected a confidence that could only be his—grabbed her ankles and lifted her legs. She felt a man's warm thighs brush up against her bottom half as a cock went into her wet vagina.

This isn't even close to the nightmares she'd been having all week about having the dildo up her throat and her fingers inside her. As Mistress Ai rode her face more vigorously, the secretions from her face coated Dalia's cheeks. Because of Mr. Sane's powerful thrusts, which also stimulated her anus, her butt plug was already moving.

Mistress' fingers were still in Dalia's hair, and she was yelling in a high-pitched, repetitive cry of approaching orgasm—at first a faint scream as she repeatedly crushed herself into Dalia's lips and tongue for what felt like a whole minute. Her body eventually became at ease.

Mistress Ai climbed off her face and gave Dalia a kiss and stroked her hair. Jerry stayed sitting and watched with curiosity as Dalia could now make out who was between her legs. Inattentive to her and absorbed with his own sensations, the older man fucked her. The idea that he was so uninterested in her and her pleasure excited Dalia and in some strange way intensified the feeling that he was inside her. Did he never get naked? Dalia loved watching him when he was still wearing his grey suit.

She could feel her own orgasm beginning to form and was almost there when Mr. Sane arched his back and walked over panting. The disadvantage of having a guy who was insensitive to her feelings, in Dalia's opinion, was that she wouldn't always be able to go.

Shortly after Jerry gave her a towel to wipe up the drips, Mr. Sane emerged from Dalia.

Mr. Sane put himself away and stood up. As he zipped up his jeans, he grumbled, "That appetizer was a complete waste. Dalia, go to the kitchen and ask Mrs. Carter when supper will be served."

While Mistress Ai was donning her kimono, Dalia decided not to request that she change. She said after going back to the kitchen, "Salute, Molly! Mr. Sane is interested to know how dinner is going."

I don't know why he cares, Molly said.

One bite at a time is all he consumes. Give him fifteen minutes to wait."

After fifteen minutes, they were all seated at a small, square dinner table. Dalia was still naked, but it hurt to sit on her butt plug. Mistress Ai was on her right, and Jerry was to her left.

Jerry hadn't spoken much tonight; perhaps he was shy. Dalia tried to talk to him, but he didn't seem to understand her. As Mistress Ai took charge of the conversation by providing news and encouraging debate about people who were acquainted to everyone present but her, Dalia felt instead restless and bored.

Mr. Sane finally pushed his chair back and stated, "With me, return to the living room. Mrs. Carter is invited to bring us coffee or other drinks for our post-dinner entertainment."

Someone, perhaps Molly, had placed a futon in the middle of the living room floor. Mr. Sane motioned for Dalia to get up on the futon. He then addressed the crowd. "I gave Dalia two homework assignments last week. One was to acclimate her anus to enduring an hour-long large butt plug. She placed a plug of that size when she stepped in tonight and has been wearing it since since, so I know she finished that one. Dalia, go on your knees and show off your butt plug for everyone."

She knelt down to show Mr. Sane her plug. She then slowly spun around so that everybody could see. When she flashed her ass with the obscene diamond in it, she relished the brief wave of embarrassment that followed.

Mr. Sane said, "She was required to learn how to deep throat a dildo as her second assignment. Dalia, did you execute it?"

She confirmed, "Mr. Sane."

"Unfortunately, I forgot to ask you to bring the dildo back so you could demonstrate your new skill. You didn't just happen to bring it, did you?"

Sir, Dalia replied, "No. "I am sorry."

"The only option is to survive. Jerry said, "No problem, Steven," when asked if he would mind if Dalia sucked his cock "After saying this, Jerry rose to his feet.

If Mr. Sane preferred to have sex while still in his clothes, Jerry was more like Mistress Ai who had undressed to play with Dalia before dinner. He leisurely took off his jacket, tie, shoes, pants, and other accoutrements until only a gold wristwatch remained. He had a nice, well-muscled torso and a narrow waist. His complexion was black with copper undertones. He held his penis in his palm and massaged it as he moved toward Dalia. All of his shyness from dinnertime had evaporated by the time he was nude and comfortable with a growing cock. Dalia thought he was an Adonis and said she had never seen a body so beautiful.

He stopped at the edge of the futon. He had a cock with a shaft that matched the rich brown colour of his body and a circumcised head that was lighter in colour with a tinge of pink. She knelt down in front of him and looked at his cock. She lifted him up in her hand, licked his entire shaft from his balls to the very tip. The dark head, then the corona, and finally the darker shaft all disappeared between her pale pink lips as she teased his slit there before slowly taking him in her mouth.

She took him slowly so they could enjoy one other and Mr. Sane and Mistress Ai, who were watching them closely, for as long as possible. She waited for her lips to touch his shaved base before extending her tongue to kiss his balls.

Mr. Sane clapped his hands and shouted, "very good Deep throating Jerry or a dildo when they're still is one thing, though. When something moves, it completely transforms. You're an expert, Jerry."

Jerry backed away from Dalia and then quickly kissed her while he was seated. She was led to a face-up position with her head pushed back and off the end of the futon as he whispered, "Lie down, babe."

After carefully lowering himself into her mouth until he was fully inside and her nose was pressed against his balls, Jerry knelt over her. After a few repetitions, he withdrew a few inches and pushed in again, this time more quickly. He applied longer, more intense strokes until her mouth was dripping with saliva, which then ran across her forehead, into her eyes, and into her hair. He was fucking her faster and deeper, the smooth sound of cock echoing in her ears, and she couldn't help but make an odd quacking noise that surprised and alarmed her.

But what a shock to be handled in such a manner! As he strained himself into her, his brown asshole flexed an inch from her eyes while his hard balls bounced. His hands were on her breasts, massaging her nipples. She vigorously stroked her pussy below where her hand had landed.

Someone was fucking her with the butt plug while dragging it about in her ass and eventually yanking it out. Hands lifted her ankles as a warm cock thrust into her ass. What else but Mr. Sane's cock could it be? She could sense the man's confidence and control in the way he thrust and gripped her. Although she was being stretched by the butt plug, the discomfort persisted. She was unable to voice her opposition, so she hummed around Jerry's big cock.

She uncomfortably stretched until she could enjoy the sensation of Mr. Sane's soft skin stroking against her anus. When Mr. Sane pushed forcefully into Dalia from below, Dalia felt it jolt her entire body into line with Jerry's cadence, and when Jerry shoved into her throat, it forced Mr. Sane deeper into her ass, heightening the feelings there.

It had to have been Mistress Ai's fingers that had pushed her hand away from her pussy and pushed into her there, even though Dalia could only see Jerry's supple and muscular ass. All of her erogenous zones were stimulated as she stroked and squeezed her nipples, sending waves of sensation crashing throughout her body.

She was filled to the brim with thick spurts before a drip escaped and ran over her cheek because she had no idea when Jerry would arrive. She observed Mistress Ai sticking her fingers into her genitalia and Mr. Sane fucking her behind after he left her. The pleasure of watching Mr. Sane and Mistress Ai, as well as the stimulation of her pussy and ass, combined with the consumption of Jerry's sperm to allow her to have an even more intense orgasm than the one she had the week before when masturbating for Mr. Sane.

Mr. Sane's hooded eyes swept over her face admiringly, but they were unable to see past the expertly applied makeup, so Dalia fixed her gaze on him. She had no interiority for him at the time because she was nowhere to be found. Good, she remarked.

Initially, she wanted to be his plaything, but later, they could talk about literature and daily life.
After he pulled out of her ass, his semen arced over her belly and splashed on her breasts, chest, and neck, causing her sphincter to tingle with pleasure. He glanced at her briefly before rising to his feet. I'm going to zip up and put myself away, he said in response. "Jerry, how's it going with that new office building? Once more, where was it? St. Louis?"
Mistress Ai and Jerry left around midnight. When Dalia and Mr. Sane returned from taking them out, he had passed out in a chair in the living room. At that precise moment, Dalia realized he had been struggling for hours to keep his cool and was now worn out. Can I help you, sir? "It was her.
Go to bed, Dalia, he said in a voice that was hardly audible above a whisper.
"I could bring you a snack or something to drink, sir. You could use my help climbing the stairs."
Get into bed.
"Sir . . ."
He yelled, "Don't try my patience, Dalia."
Yes, Sir, she said. Sir, good night.
He remained silent.
Her overnight bag was next to the door of her room. She pulled out some toiletries and hung some things on the closet rod

before heading to the restroom. She filled the bath with warm water and took a long soak, which helped her sore anus.

When she tried to fall asleep, nothing happened. It had been an overly eventful evening. She had alternately been present and absent, the centre of attention and only a tool for their use. Everyone had penetrated her; they had perforated and slimed her, used and abused her; it had been disgusting, but the disgust had made her want it. Unexpectedly, they had respected and loved her even when she had been a thing for them. They had been considerate enough to attend to both their demands and hers after understanding them.

But Mrs. Sane alarmed her. During the two evenings she spent with him, she had never seen somebody as worn out as he had been.

A memory from when she was only nine came back to her in an instant. That exhausted, thin, and pale her mother had gotten as she battled breast cancer. It appeared as though a huge hand was encircling Dalia's heart.

Which medication did she observe in Mr. Sane's kitchen cabinet, and what was its name? She pulled her phone out of her bag and searched for "Gleevec."

She read and reread online sites from three in the morning until dawn.

At eight, Mr. Sane invited her to breakfast, which he was preparing himself, rather than tying her up.
When the mood hits, I'm not a horrible cook, he admitted. Was it just in her mind, or did he seem a little more cordial this morning?
As she sipped her coffee, she observed him frying bacon, bread, and sausage. He brought her a plate that was stuffed full of food.
She said, "Mr. Sane, this looks delicious, but it's about four times as much as I usually eat." Will it offend you if I only eat one bite of each item?
He said, "I'd take you to the red room of pain and cane you if I were Christian Grey."
Dalia shouted, "Thank God you're not Christian Grey, Sir. "I'd be a sow after two weeks with him."
I'm not an addict to food, he insisted. I'm not sure I could eat as much as you do.
Following a minute of silence, Mr. Sane said: "Your tales were excellent. They are genuinely talented, and it would be wise to get to know them. They brought back painful memories of awkward teenage years and embarrassing incidents from my own school days. What are you writing right now?"
She shared her thoughts with him regarding the subway panhandlers.
I like it, he remarked.

Do you think the girl will be saved by a wealthy man who supports her in exchange for sex?"

Dalia pronounced, "The concept is too idealistic. That would not be the case."

Despite its strange, cutting cough, Mr. Sane chuckled, and it was obvious what he was laughing at. Dalia was both surprised and overjoyed.

She remarked: "Even though I want to save her, I think she has to go down further before she can climb out and get away. Prostitution. possibly using drugs perhaps more On the streets, homeless people endure terrible things."

He replied with regret, "I guess so. Funny how people often feel worse off in fiction than they do in reality.

Without you, Sir, my life would be very challenging."

You'll be alright. It might be a bit more difficult."

May I enquire further about you, Sir? Dalia asked. What do you do when you're not reading, gambling with other people's money, or mistreating the bodies of women?

There's not much to say, he said.

I'm a very dull man. I read, have lunches with friends, and watch TV."

Have you got kids?

Why do you want to know, he inquired?

I'm intrigued, said Dalia. "We are linked together. It makes reasonable for others to be curious about you."

He suggested you ask another question.

Do you have brothers or siblings?

"Dalia!"

"You questioned, "Sir, are you the only human in the world?" If you are, please let me know immediately away."

"I relish my time alone. I have you, in any case."

But, Sir, you don't treat me like a lover, a friend, or even a family member."

We've talked about writing...

Not even "Sir, do you have a family?" will you be said.

She responded, "Our contract doesn't state I have to be honest with you.

"Perhaps you require more right now, Sir, than is included in the contract. Even though I've been incredibly thrilled since becoming your sexual object for a short while, I'm scared for you."

You say you're worried "about your well-being, Sir. your lingering leukaemia."

How did you discover that?

"I haven't been nosy, sir. You asked me to grab some Advil last week, but I couldn't ignore how fatigued you were, and I saw that you were also taking Gleevec."

"If I die, Mr. Sane said icily, you'll be taken care of. There's no need to worry."

She went into a rage. Do you really think that all I'm concerned with is getting paid, sir? "She inquired.

He stated that "you wouldn't be here" if I wasn't paying.

"She said, "You're convinced I regard you as just a James, and I'm just a whore to you." Due to this, you've never kissed me. A kiss is not given to a whore. You don't touch her more than you have to."

I don't think of you as a whore, Dalia.

"So please quit treating me like one, Mr. Sane. Treat me as if I can care about your well-being even though our relationship is strictly professional."

Mr. Sane appeared to be gathering his patience as he dipped his head and pinched the bridge of his nose.

"Go home," he told Dalia. "Don't worry about me. I'll be fine."

Dalia thought he wasn't going to be okay. If she understood what she had read, his leukaemia was progressing, and she was concerned. You're not a doctor, Dalia, he said, "Your symptoms, Sir." "Go home."

Should I come back on Friday? "She questioned.

Yes, he answered. "Next Friday. Further information will be supplied."

On January 21, Mr. Sane wrote Dalia to inform her that she wouldn't be required that weekend. She could wait another week, but she was disappointed because she had been hoping to once again become Mr. Sane's and possibly more of his friends' favourite sex toy. Before buying a vibrator from a sex shop in the city centre, she played with the dildo and butt-plugs he had given her while being unaware of the salesperson's rabid expression.

Dalia became concerned when Mr. Sane had to cancel again the following week. She alternated between believing he was leaving her and believing his condition was getting worse. She received her rent payment and a cheque for living expenses as usual the following week, but he didn't invite her to his house. She wrote him a letter saying, "I hope you're doing well, Sir, and that I haven't upset you." I eagerly look forward our meetups.

He ignored my email message. But the idea of calling him frightened her.

She wrote Mr. Sane once more the next week, asking if they could discuss it if he was angry with her. That is the right move to make in both business and personal interactions.

He responded on February 6 by saying, "I'm not mad at you." When you are required, you will be notified. Your assistance will continue.

"This narrative is a huge departure for you," Mr. Stone, Dalia's advanced fiction writing class instructor, said. Dalia had felt honoured to be accepted into his class because he was a tough novelist in his fifties with chiselled features. It was Tuesday, February 11 and it had been more than three weeks since she had last seen Mr. Sane.

I hope it's okay, Mr. Stone, Dalia said. When he called her into his office after class, she was afraid he would inform her that her account of the subway panhandler was untrue. She had skillfully detailed how her story, a svelte sixty-two-year-old man, had snatched her up anally and orally at the location where Stella had executed her first ruse.

Naturally, Mr. Stone said, it is acceptable. "In reality, it's great. I do have some concerns, however they are more about you than the story. Of course, we all know about your father and your situation. I sincerely apologize for everything. Such a big loss, and you're not even to blame. It occurred to me after reading your account that it might be a result of your own experience of abandonment or the loss of your family and/or support network."

THE END

CPSIA information can be obtained
at www.ICGtesting.com
Printed in the USA
LVHW050957251122
733913LV00003B/8

9 781804 345771